The Transatlantic Conspiracy

The Transatlantic Conspiracy

G.D. FALKSEN

Published in the United States by Soho Teen
an imprint of
Soho Press, Inc.
853 Broadway
New York, NY 10003

Library of Congress Cataloging-in-Publication Data
Falksen, G. D. (Geoffrey D.), 1982–
The transatlantic conspiracy / G. D. Falksen.

ISBN 978-1-61695-814-5
eISBN 978-1-61695-418-5

1. Railroad trains—Fiction. 2. Conspiracies—Fiction.
3. Mystery and detective stories.
4. Love—Fiction. 5. Science fiction. I. Title

PZ7.1.F352 2016 DDC [Fic]—dc23 2015031406

Interior art (pages 28–29, 68–69, 118–119, 186–187, 216–217)
by Nat Iwata

Octopus: A. Pollock

Interior design by Janine Agro, Soho Press, Inc.

Printed in the United States of America

10 9 8 7 6 5 4 3 2 1

*My thanks to the incredible team at
Soho Press for all their hard work and dedication.*

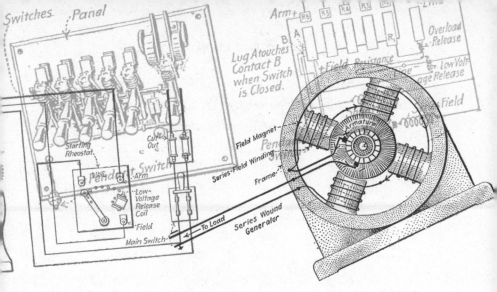

To: Miss Rosalind Wallace
Exham House, London, England
25 May, 1908

My dearest Rosalind. Warmest regards from
your mother and me. Hope you have been
enjoying your stay in London, etc. Send our
warmest regards to Lord Exham and his wife,
etc. Be sure not to catch cold in the rain, etc.
Your mother reminds you to put on a hat out
of doors, etc.

Wonderful news that I know will excite you.
You are required back in America at once. And as
my Transatlantic Express departs Hamburg on
its inaugural voyage in two weeks, I have decided
that you will represent the family on the journey.
Your ticket will be sent along from the London
office in a few days. No need to thank me.

Chapter One

Do remember to dress respectably. The train will carry only one hundred passengers in all, and that includes Second Class. The public will judge you. Have a wonderful journey!

Your loving father,
Alexander Wallace

○   ○   ○

Rosalind Wallace lowered her father's telegram, speechless. She had always known that her holiday in London would have to end, but in the excitement of the social season, it had all gone by so quickly.

And now Father wanted her to return home? And on his underwater railway, no less?

She took a deep breath. Yet another one of his publicity stunts, no doubt. Rosalind knew what he was up to. It made her want to scream. She felt the eyes of her friend and hostess, Cecily de Vere, watching her from across the room.

Cecily was at the window, feeding her pair of songbirds. She was rather like those birds, Rosalind realized: perennially fair and pretty, chirping delight at everything around her, even the familiar. And why not? If this were Rosalind's home, she too would delight in the gilded birdcage and the rich parlor with its endless rows of clocks. She *had* delighted in it all.

Now her stay here—arranged almost entirely at Cecily's insistence—was at its telegrammed end.

Cecily's infectious smile melted into a frown. "Is something the matter, Rose? Not bad news, is it?"

Rosalind marched over and held the paper out to her friend. "It's from my father. He's asked me to return home."

Cecily's face fell. "What horrid news!"

Rosalind could do little more than offer a sad smile.

"I simply cannot imagine London without you," Cecily stated. "Say it's not so. Has it already been three months? Do you really have to return home?"

"Father is insistent," Rosalind answered grimly.

Home meant Pittsburgh, a place she'd almost managed to forget while in London. Home was a reflection of Father: always practical, never glamorous. He preferred to keep his family close to his steel investments. Rosalind would only be able to justify a week or two in New York City before being dragged back to the land of smoke and steel mills. Either that or she could summer with Mother on Long Island, which was its own bundle of nonsense, none of it a substitute for the London Season.

She sighed and sat in the chair beside Cecily.

"And after all the trouble we went to introducing you into respectable society . . ." Cecily's voice trailed off. She brightened and took Rose by the hand. "Don't worry, Rose. It only means that Charles and I will have to visit you in America. It will be such fun, truly it will. I could . . ." She paused, turning back to the caged birds, her eyes sparkling.

"What are you thinking?" Rosalind asked.

"I could accompany you!" Cecily exclaimed.

Rosalind dropped her friend's hand. She would love

that, but she imagined Lord and Lady Exham might have something to say about it.

"I've always wanted to see New York," Cecily continued.

"Cecily—"

"And cowboys."

"Cecily!" Rosalind couldn't help but match Cecily's grin. She waved a hand to catch her friend's attention and draw it away from the birds.

Cecily blinked a few times. "Hmm? When must you leave us? You have until the middle of summer, surely."

"Two weeks. And then I must depart for Germany."

"Germany?" Cecily's delicate features twisted at the suggestion. "Whatever for?"

"Father's great Transatlantic Express," Rosalind grumbled. "I'm to represent the family on the inaugural journey. He does this sort of thing, places this responsibility upon me. The train departs from Hamburg, so to Hamburg I must go."

"How utterly abhorrent."

Rosalind shrugged. "I suppose I should put a bright face on it. I'd rather like to visit Germany. Sometime. Not now, of course, but sometime."

"Yes, during the summer, perhaps," Cecily said, "after the Season finishes." She flashed an impish smile over her shoulder. "Mother and I could offer to take you there, under our care. And then you wouldn't have to go back to America at all, would you?"

So incorrigible. Rosalind laughed. "I don't think my father would agree. I suspect that my return to America is more about the railway than it is about me."

"Whatever do you mean?" Cecily asked.

Oh, what to say? Rosalind thought. Indeed, what *could* she say? That Father had used her and her mother to advertise his blasted trains for as long as she could remember? That the first photograph snapped of her as an infant had shown her in her father's arms as he rode a locomotive his own engineers had warned might explode without warning? That she sometimes wondered if she'd rather been born a shopgirl if it meant having a father who considered her something other than a convenient business tool?

Rosalind realized that her hands had become fists. She forced herself to relax. "My father has performed some remarkable feats of engineering these past few years—"

"Like that railway bridge across your Hudson River?" Cecily interrupted.

Ah yes, the Fort Washington Bridge connecting Manhattan and New Jersey. She had been thinking of just the same thing. She and Cecily always seemed to do that, to think of the same thing at the same time. Until now, it had always made her laugh.

"A perfect example," Rosalind said. "The papers all claimed it couldn't be done. Everyone said it would collapse the first time a train rolled across it."

"Only it didn't," Cecily said.

Rosalind chuckled. "And for that I am grateful. As a publicity stunt, my father took the first train across . . . with Mother and me in tow. To show there was nothing to fear. Now he's built this underwater railway, and I'm certain the newspapers are predicting disaster. My presence on the train is my father's way of reassuring the public."

"Your father would let you drown?" Cecily exclaimed, aghast.

"I'm not going to *drown*," Rosalind said, rolling her eyes. "Father's no fool, believe me. He has every confidence in his train. *I* have every confidence in it. He's just using me to remind everyone else that they ought to have confidence in it as well."

Cecily clucked her tongue. "Well, public confidence or not, I do not approve of him spiriting my best friend away. He should have waited until autumn."

"Annoyed that the peasants are interfering with your plans, Cecily?" Rosalind teased.

"Yes," Cecily said. Then she caught herself. "No. I mean . . . That is to say . . . not that you're a peasant, Rose. I mean, you *are* a peasant—"

"Oh, thanks," Rosalind interrupted.

Cecily's face reddened. "But you're *my* peasant," she finished, "and that makes all the difference, doesn't it?"

Rosalind laughed at the joke. Still, a part of her knew that it was true. She was no de Vere. Her paternal grandfather had been a penniless steelworker from Scotland; even her mother could trace her family's wealth and status only as far back as the American Revolution. Centuries of aristocratic blood ran through Cecily's veins. The miracle was that it didn't matter to Cecily or to her family. Cecily even made a point of giving her friend a proper introduction into London Society.

True, Rosalind had gotten a taste of debutante balls and socials and cotillions in New York. Her self-made father's wealth and accomplishments had forced even old-money families to accept the upstart Wallaces. "Accept," of course—not "welcome." And that was the difference. Compared with London, New York felt so false and pretentious, so competitive. Members of Cecily's class knew that they had nothing to lose by welcoming Rosalind: she could never possibly be one of them; she didn't pose a threat. She really *was* Cecily's peasant.

And right now, as far as Rosalind was concerned, that was wonderful. It was far preferable to being a pawn in her father's advertising campaign.

"Well, I for one am not about to sit here and do nothing while your beast of a father—I do beg your pardon— drags you back to America,"

Cecily said, breaking the silence. She flashed a conspiratorial grin.

"Are you going to write him a strongly worded letter?" Rosalind asked dryly.

Cecily stood. "No. The time for strongly worded letters has passed. Now is the time for action." She grabbed Rosalind by the hand and pulled her to the door. "We're going to tell Charles. He'll know what to do."

❂   ❂   ❂

Viselike handholding often accompanied Cecily's stubborn will. Rosalind stumbled along behind her friend through the upstairs of the de Veres' palatial town house. She nearly collided with a member of the staff, her eyes drawn to the old oil paintings, the marble statues, the suit of armor transplanted from the family's ancestral home in Devon.

Again her heart squeezed at the thought of how much she'd miss it here. Exham House had been built in the eighteenth century, its furnishings, like the Exham title, passed down through the generations—so stark a contrast to Rosalind's own home, where everything had to be newer, better, and more expensive, no matter how hideous it was.

In the upstairs study they found Cecily's elder brother seated at the desk, busily scribbling in a sketchbook. At first he did not notice them, or pretended not to.

Charles was only a year older than Cecily, about Rosalind's age. But he had grown remarkably well since Rosalind had first met him—ages ago, when Father's great aquatic railroad had been in its infancy, back when Charles and Cecily's father, the Earl of Exham, had first approached Father about getting in on a transportation scheme in Canada. Rosalind had been very much a girl then, and Charles had been very much a boy.

Now Charles had his father's sturdy build and the strong de Vere jaw. His sandy hair was well kept, a few shades fairer than his sister's luxuriant chestnut. And he dressed as only a young Englishman could. But what she loved most about him was his conversation. Unlike the boys at home, he had a brain.

"Charles," Cecily announced, "we have a terrible problem. You are going to stop drawing and help us solve it."

Charles looked up from his sketchbook with a frown.

Rosalind smiled to herself: even in confusion—or perhaps especially in confusion—Charles was charming, a lion who thought himself a house cat, majestic by all appearances but adorable when he became tangled in a ball of string.

"Cecily, whatever are you going on about? Good morning, Rosalind. Has my sister gone quite mad?"

"Not very mad, no," Rosalind said shyly.

"Rose's father is demanding that she return to America." Cecily's tone made it sound as if Rosalind were on the verge of being kidnapped. "We must put a stop to it."

Charles blinked a few times and shook his head, mouthing a few words silently as he tried to formulate a proper reply. "You're . . . leaving?"

Rosalind nodded. "Unfortunately—"

"She is!" Cecily interjected. "She's to go back on the Transatlantic Express. In two weeks! From Germany!" She turned to Rosalind. "Your father could have at least done the decent thing and sent you home on a proper English boat."

"Ship," Charles corrected.

"Hush," Cecily muttered, rolling her eyes.

"The Transatlantic Express?" Charles continued, ignoring his sister. "Rosalind, you're leaving on your father's train?"

"Yes, I am," Rosalind said. "I shall be representing the family. It's my daughterly duty."

Charles furrowed his brow. Suddenly he snapped his fingers and leapt to his feet. "Well, dash it all," he said. "Cecily and I will simply have to accompany you."

"We will?" Cecily asked, eyes wide.

"We will," Charles said, meeting her gaze.

Cecily turned back to Rosalind and nodded firmly. "We will," she echoed, breaking into a wide smile, as if this had been her plan all along.

"I . . . You will?" Rosalind stammered.

The thought of having Cecily—and Charles—accompany her on the unwanted journey home excited her, but experience had shown that Cecily's enthusiasm often outmatched her willpower. Like the time in April when she had insisted she would remain at Rosalind's side for the duration of the ball (she forgot whose) . . . only to run off with some Russian officer for half the evening. At least Cecily had apologized for it when she returned: she was just easily distracted.

But Charles was another matter. Charles was reluctant to make promises, and he kept his word when he did. He'd promised Rosalind flowers for her birthday, and so he'd gone out in the middle of a thunderstorm to fetch them. The memory of how he stood in the library, soaking wet and holding a bouquet of roses, still made Rosalind smile. They had been yellow roses, for friendship, but even so . . .

"But what will Mummy and Daddy say?" Cecily asked. "Surely they'd never allow it."

Charles frowned a little, staring off into the distance. Then he snapped his fingers again. "You just leave them to me. I don't know why it never occurred to me before, but the maiden voyage of the Transatlantic Express . . . well, it's the chance of a lifetime. The event of the century."

"Oh, nonsense, Charles," Cecily said. "The century's just begun. There's no telling what will come."

"To compare with crossing the ocean on an underwater train?" Rosalind countered.

"A fair point," Cecily said.

"Even if it's not the event of the century, we've been cooped up in London long enough," Charles remarked. "And I for one could do with a grand adventure. And what better place for an adventure than America?"

"Iceland?" Rosalind teased.

Rosalind did wonder what Charles would really think of America when he got there. America was . . . well, it was America. Unruly. Troublesome. Thanks to her father, Rosalind had crisscrossed it from top to bottom and from east to west; she had seen the heights of its glory and the depths of its vulgarity. Besides, though she truly loved it, it was nothing compared with London, the heart of the world's greatest empire. What if Charles went and found her homeland disappointing? And what if he found *her* disappointing? In England she was an "exotic American." In America she was . . . well, an unruly troublemaker, if one asked Mother.

"We'd be fools to miss the chance, wouldn't we?" Charles continued. "Anyone important on the Continent will be onboard, and I daresay we'll see a few familiar faces from England as well."

"I shouldn't think so," Cecily muttered. "Leaving London in the middle of the Season to visit Germany?" She shuddered at the thought. "How very Continental." She caught Rosalind's eye, as if suddenly remembering her friend, and brightened. "Until we *leave* the Continent, of course. Charles is right."

Rosalind wasn't sure. Continental or not, it was strange to abandon London, to travel to Germany, to take a train to America . . . a train that may very well sink and end up on the ocean floor. And of course, Father wasn't trying to attract the English anyway—at least not yet. The maiden journey was above all a publicity stunt, and one intended mostly for the benefit of the Germans and the French. Besides, the British had the finest passenger liners in the world: What use did they have for a transatlantic train?

"Charles?" Rosalind spoke informally, which had become her habit over the past few months. Mother would be scandalized if she ever found out. "It's very kind of you to offer, but are you certain you want to go . . . ?" She bit her tongue before ending the question: *With me?* She would have sounded foolish asking that.

"Just think of it," Charles replied, rubbing his hands together. "The glamour, the excitement, the—"

"The Germans," Cecily interrupted, scrunching up her face. "The Belgians."

"Don't speak ill of the Belgians, Cecily," Charles scolded. "They're a splendid people." His tone lightened. "I thought you'd appreciate my impetuousness. No, but I am adamant about this. It's going to be great fun. Though I daresay you'll have to make due with a little anonymity. I rather suspect that in traveling with dear Rosalind, we'll be eclipsed by her."

"How do you imagine that?" Rosalind asked. She could hardly picture Cecily being eclipsed by anyone. And certainly Charles was . . . memorable. *I'm staring at him again*, she realized, looking away.

"Rosalind, as the daughter of the railway owner, you will be the centerpiece of the entire journey," Charles said, almost sounding sorry for her. "As your father no doubt intends."

"No doubt," Rosalind agreed.

"I suspect we will have to struggle to be paid any mind by anyone," Charles said. He sighed in mock regret, teasing his sister. "However are we to make due with anonymity?"

"Oh, I see," Cecily said. She looked off vacantly for a moment and added, "Ah. That puts it in a very different light." Then all at once, she was her old self again. "And that is quite terrible. Making due with anonymity. And at a great social event!"

Charles grinned at her. "So, we'll accompany Rosalind, then?"

"We shall," Cecily replied, squeezing Rosalind's hand.

"Will your parents approve?" Rosalind asked.

"Leave Mother and Father to me," Charles said. He winked at Cecily. "I'll put it to them properly. By tomorrow morning, they'll be all for it. I give you my word." He headed for the door. There he paused and turned back. Looking at Rosalind, he said, "This is going to be great fun."

Once Charles's footsteps had faded downstairs, Rosalind turned to Cecily. "Seven days on a train? 'Great fun'? Has your brother lost his mind?"

"An underwater train," Cecily corrected, giggling. She took Rosalind's free hand and squeezed that one, too.

"How can you dislike traveling on trains? Your father's made his fortune building them."

Rosalind sighed. That was precisely the reason she *disliked* trains, though it would be impossible to explain that to Cecily. What could she say of her childhood, the small eternities on her father's railway cars, rattling to this town and that; her father always on the move, always encouraging the local city heads to invest in newer, bigger, better, and above all more expensive transportation networks?

"Oh, if my father were your father, Cecily," she said, "you would understand."

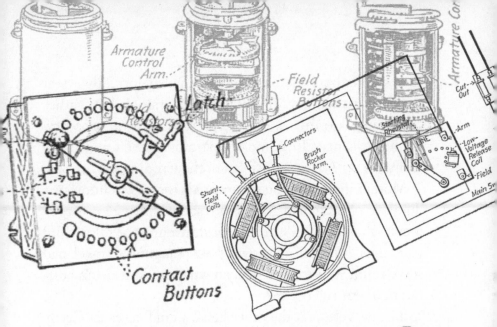

Armature Control Arm · Latch · Field Resistor Buttons · Field Resistors · Connectors · Brush Rocker Arm · Shunt Field Coils · Starting Rheostat · Armature Co · Cut-Out · Arm · Low-Voltage Release Coil · Field · Main Sw · Contact Buttons

How Charles had managed it was a mystery to Rosalind, but by the next morning Lord and Lady Exham had thrown their wholehearted support behind the idea. They even went so far as to agree that the three might travel unchaperoned—or rather, that Cecily and Rosalind would be chaperoned by Charles. It made a degree of sense, if only a marginal one: Lord and Lady Exham would never allow their daughter to travel without supervision, so of course they wanted her older brother to accompany her.

But Rosalind wasn't a member of the family. Neither she nor Charles was married. Charles was the last person who should be chaperoning her.

But why question the decision? This was exactly what Rosalind had wanted.

And of course Lord and Lady Exham knew

Chapter Two

that she had traveled unaccompanied before, always at her father's request. It was unconventional, but Father regarded his trains as more or less his private property: so, he reasoned, Rosalind wasn't alone. Each and every train worker was responsible for chaperoning her.

Mother disagreed, on the grounds that it was improper. The two of them had gotten into some truly vicious arguments about it. But Father's pride would not allow him to budge. His attitude toward his daughter's travel had served him well in America, so why should it be any different under the ocean?

The de Veres, on the other hand, would never let Cecily travel alone. They did not agree with Rosalind's father's unorthodox "New World" views, and though they feigned respect for them, Charles's presence was a necessity. He would accompany the girls for their safety. A kind thought, but really, being a young and unmarried man, Charles wasn't quite a typical chaperone. An older aunt would have been more fitting. That they agreed to Charles's plan did strike Rosalind as rather odd. But, she reasoned, since she and the de Vere siblings would spend the entire journey in the safety of the train, and be met by her family upon arrival in New York City, there was little chance of danger or mishap.

Unless something went wrong with the train, of course. But no chaperone could help them if they sank.

❂   ❂   ❂

The next two weeks passed in a flash of preparation and packing.

Cecily, of course, insisted that she and Rosalind have several new dresses made for the "event"—she refused to call it a "journey"—though Rosalind did wonder about her friend's tastes. Cecily refused anything less than matching patterns and designs for the two of them, and while the dresses were very pretty, Rosalind had her doubts about looking exactly like her companion, their chaperone's other ward. Cecily was convinced that it would be much more fun if they looked "like twins."

Although Rosalind thought they looked silly, she had no desire to protest. She would have the company of her best friend and her best friend's brother on this voyage. And then, there was one dress in blue and gold that Rosalind particularly liked . . . and that Charles seemed to admire when he saw it, if his stunned silence was any indication. If only Cecily hadn't bought one to match. The last thing Rosalind wanted was for Charles to think she looked like his sister. But maybe that was Cecily's intention all along.

No. Rosalind was overthinking, as always. It was best not to think; it was best to prepare. Father's offices in London had already sent the travel papers. She was a very lucky girl. She could have been traveling alone.

◊   ◊   ◊

The newly built Transatlantic Railway Station in Hamburg was like nothing Rosalind had ever seen in her life—and she had seen more than her fair share of grand railroad stations over the years. All the boring professional commentary tended to ruin the simple appreciation of their architectural beauty. That and the waiting crowds of newspaper reporters that always seemed to be on hand whenever Father had taken her "sightseeing."

There was something of the old Grand Central Station in the railway's private depot at Hamburg, and the façade was reminiscent of the Gare du Nord in Paris; though perhaps it would have been better to say that the Louvre had been its inspiration.

The interior was a glamorous palace of polished wood, marble, and brass. Countless waiting rooms, restaurants, and parlors for entertainment were spread out alongside the grand concourse that led from the entrance to the ticket windows, and finally to the platform. Despite the tremendous grandeur of the surroundings, the passengers struck Rosalind as unimpressed, more focused on one another. The crowd was thick and spirited, with people pushing and shoving in a desperate attempt to catch sight of some dignitary or actress. Cecily had been right to call this an "event."

Rosalind laughed at the crowd's antics, but at the same time she found herself craning her neck to hear passersby as they spoke, searching for any hint of an American accent. Perhaps she was homesick. She pressed on toward the train, arm in arm with Cecily. The two were dressed identically except for Cecily's oversized hat. Rosalind was very grateful Cecily hadn't insisted upon *that* match. The mass of silk and feathers looked like an animal that might pounce at any moment.

Charles followed behind them, giving instructions to his valet, Harris, a rather serious-looking fellow who, as ever, wore a dark suit and gray trousers. He nodded slightly at everything Charles said, as if to reassure his master that he was listening, though for all Rosalind knew, he may not have been. Cecily's maid—a young girl named Doris—brought up the rear, seemingly ignored by everyone but Rosalind. If they'd been leaving Pittsburgh instead of Hamburg, Rosalind might have struck up a conversation with the girl. But how could she? In London she'd learned: engaging the servants for any reason other than servitude simply wasn't done. At least, not in the de Vere household.

Besides, Rosalind had to look after herself. She'd already been very nearly stampeded by a trio of newspapermen in pursuit of some hapless theater star.

"It's rather exciting, isn't it?" Cecily whispered.

"It's certainly rather *something*," Rosalind answered. "I've never seen such a crowd."

"That's a good thing, though, isn't it?" Cecily said, her eyes darting. "It means that your father is going to be fabulously successful and build more of these all across the world! And that means you'll be able to come and visit us all the time." She paused for a moment. "Or so I assume."

Rosalind laughed. She wanted to believe it. What if it was true? What if the railway really was such a success? Father might become the talk of Europe. And beyond. And if that happened . . . well, anything could happen. Father might become so successful he wouldn't need to parade his family in front of the press every time he built a new railroad or developed a new locomotive engine. *I might be able to do what I want*, Rosalind thought. *To go where I want.* A rich father preoccupied with his success might let his daughter do as she pleased, regardless of what her Mother thought about it. Rosalind would have to marry eventually, but there would be plenty of time to travel the world with Cecily before then. With Charles as their chaperone . . .

"Oh, my word!" Cecily suddenly exclaimed.

"What?" Rosalind asked, alarmed.

Cecily reached out with her free arm and pointed across the chamber.

"It's the Kaiser!"

"The . . ." Rosalind craned her head and lifted herself on tiptoes to try to get a better look over the crowd. "Where?"

It took her a few moments of searching, but her eyes eventually fell upon a stern figure standing high above the swarm, at a podium directly in front of the great gilded archway that led to the railway platform, which was concealed behind a velvet curtain.

The emperor of Germany looked regal and imperious with his white uniform, a polished breastplate, and a proud upturned mustache. So much finery. Her father would have worn a plain suit and a hat. Unlike Cecily and Charles, the Kaiser struck Rosalind as hopelessly old-fashioned, almost childlike: he was either a medieval knight playing at being a head of state or a head of state playing at being a knight, and Rosalind didn't know which was worse. It was rather the state of monarchs in the modern world, she realized. They were overgrown children who clung to the past at all costs, afraid of being swept away on a tidal wave of progress.

"What's the smile for, Rose?" Cecily whispered.

"I'm just excited about getting aboard," Rosalind lied. But she almost laughed out loud. In spite of her enchantment with the London social scene, maybe she was more American than she'd been willing to admit. Father would certainly be proud if that was the case.

After a pause, the Kaiser began to address the crowd in guttural German. Rosalind knew she was in for a hideously long and boring speech. For a moment she didn't know whether to regret her poor understanding of the language or to be glad of it.

"Is he saying anything important?" she asked Cecily, whose German was far better than her own.

Cecily listened, lips pursed. Then she shrugged. "Oh, the usual. Momentous occasion, the glory of the event, the joining of two great nations bound together by, oh, I don't know, probably a mutual love of eagles or something."

"Tush," Rosalind said, clucking her tongue at Cecily, but she smirked. When she turned back to the podium, her view was blocked. The three reporters who'd been chasing the starlet had planted themselves, more or less as one, directly in front of her.

"Um . . ." Rosalind began, drawing back a pace.

"Please to excuse me, Fräulein," one of the men said, speaking in heavily accented English, "but am I correct to be thinking that you are Fräulein Wallace?"

The question startled her. She'd prepared herself for being recognized once aboard the train, but with all the chaos, she had not expected anyone *here* to recognize her, least of all some newspaperman. Still, she knew her father would want her to be honest, and surely there was no harm in confirming her identity.

"I am, yes," she said. "But how did you know that?"

A second reporter pushed his way forward and touched the brim of his bowler hat.

"John Gervais, Miss," he said. "*The Times*. We recognized you from your picture."

He held up a copy of his own newspaper, dated three days earlier, and offered it to Rosalind for inspection. She took the paper and stared in astonishment at the sight of her own face—lacking clarity due to the print, but more or less recognizable—set to one side of the front page, under the heading INDUSTRIALIST'S DAUGHTER TO ACCOMPANY MAIDEN VOYAGE OF UNDERWATER TRAIN.

Rosalind seethed silently, biting her tongue to avoid an outburst. Father really *had* used her to advertise the train—and in a very public way that he'd also chosen to keep from her. How dare he? *How dare he?*

But she kept smiling and said, with great self-control, "Oh my goodness. I hadn't expected him to . . . *advertise it*." The last words were spoken through clenched teeth, despite her best efforts.

With a quick, angry motion she passed the newspaper to Cecily, who arched her eyebrows in an appropriately disapproving manner. Charles took notice and leaned over his sister's shoulder to read the article. He looked at Rosalind and then back at the picture a few times.

"It's rather a good likeness, actually," he murmured.

Rosalind sighed.

Cecily's eyes were on the newsprint. "We're mentioned

as well! 'Miss Wallace is expected to be traveling in the company of Viscount Charles and Lady Cecily de Vere, children of the Earl of Exham . . .'"

"Well, fancy that," Charles said.

The third reporter pushed his way forward with a large camera and tripod. "Mademoiselle," he said, "if you would be so kind, perhaps a photograph of you? Of you and the lady and the gentleman?"

"Um, well, I . . ." Rosalind began. She felt rather dubious about the whole idea of having her name in some newspaper, let alone being photographed then and there. And how could she ask poor Cecily and Charles to join in when her father had been so uncouth as to have their names printed along with hers? Had Lord and Lady Exham been warned? Rosalind very much doubted it. But before she could protest, Cecily seized her arm in excitement.

"Marvelous!" her friend exclaimed. Cecily quickly tilted her chin and struck a pose at Rosalind's side.

A torrent of bright flashes exploded in front of Rosalind's eyes, followed by the smell of burning powder. It suddenly seemed that every news photographer in Europe had descended upon them through supernatural means. She blinked, purple dots swimming before her eyes. It was all she could do to manage a smile.

"Any words on your father's venture?" asked the German reporter, producing a notepad and pencil. "Do you find it exciting? Frightening? Thrilling?"

"Well, I—" Rosalind began.

"Do you believe that the Transatlantic Railway will

replace the ocean liner?" the Englishman from *The Times* interrupted.

"I hardly think—"

"Does your family dislike sea travel?"

"No, of course not—"

"Is your father declaring war on steamships?"

"Now, look here," Rosalind grumbled, "that is absolutely absurd—"

"So you doubt your father's latest creation?" someone else asked.

"Of course not!" Rosalind snapped. She felt cornered, as if surrounded by predators. "I have every confidence—"

"Why has your father sent you alone?" asked yet another reporter. "Why isn't he here to accompany you?"

The question gave Rosalind pause, for it had been troubling her as well, though she reminded herself this wasn't the first time he hadn't joined her. She reflexively knew not to frown; she heard her mother's voice in her head telling her never to do such a thing in public. And good Lord, there were a lot of reporters. Too many. How could the photographers refill their flash powder so quickly? And what must the Kaiser think? For all she knew, she was interrupting his very important, very German speech, right?

"That is a silly question," she said, holding her head high in the manner that Mother would have wanted her to. "My father is in America, overseeing every preparation for our safe arrival. In order to leave from Germany on his underwater train's maiden voyage, he would have had to travel to Europe by ship. And how could he possibly have taken a ship when he is pioneering suboceanic rail travel?"

It was a contrived answer that likely had no basis in fact, but at least it sounded decent. She'd had lots of practice making similar pronouncements.

And now Cecily had them all smiling and laughing with her poses. With any luck, the papers would print Cecily's picture alone and leave Rosalind out of it.

The only one who wasn't smiling was Charles's man, Harris. He stood to one side, watching the crowd. Rubbing her eyes, Rosalind noticed his ever-dour face forming a distinct grimace. He looked in Charles's direction and jerked his head toward something or someone in the crowd. Rosalind followed with her eyes but could make out only a mass of more or less identical bowlers and top hats.

One stood out from the crowd, however, because below it a pair of eyes locked with hers. A man with a mustache, in a brown suit and matching bowler, was staring at her. He quickly turned away and disappeared.

Now Charles was frowning, too. When he noticed Rosalind, he smiled again. But it was forced. Strange. He was troubled by whatever he had seen; Rosalind was certain of it. Had he been troubled by that strange man with the mustache? Charles leaned over and whispered something in Cecily's ear, but the newspapermen and photographers were still making far too much noise for Rosalind to hear any of it.

"Does your father advocate an alliance between Germany and America?" asked one, raising his voice at Rosalind.

What a silly question, she thought.

"I would imagine that my father, being a man of science, would also be a tremendous advocate of progress, industry, and commerce," she replied, somewhat tersely. "The German government had terribly good sense in partnering with him in this venture. If the French had taken him up on the offer, I've no doubt we would be departing from somewhere in Brittany. And I also have no doubt that my father's business is his and not mine, and I have no further answers to give you."

She smiled, and the smile wasn't phony. No, she considered it to be a rather good answer, good enough at least to placate this idiotic rabble. Father had often remarked that she made a fine public speaker. Had she been born a boy, he'd told her, he would send her to study law or stand for political office. The compliment was comical, in a way— at least from his point of view. He never understood why she became so incensed at such comments. Progress, as far as he was concerned, was to be determined by men.

"Come on," Rosalind muttered to Cecily, "let's get aboard before they depart without us and we're left here with this mob of reporters."

"A splendid idea," Cecily agreed.

o   o   o

At the platform, Rosalind glanced over her shoulder. Doris was right behind them, though a few people back in the crowd. Rosalind smiled and motioned for the girl to join them properly, for surely there was no harm in it. As she did so, Rosalind realized that she'd lost track of Charles and Harris.

"Cecily," she said, stopping short. She shook free of

Cecily's arm, looped within hers, and whirled around on her tiptoes. "Can you see Charles?"

"Oh, don't worry," she said, patting Rosalind's back. "He's gone off to telegraph Daddy about some business. Nothing important, of course. Something dull, dull, dull, no doubt. I expect he'll meet us on the train."

"Ah," Rosalind said. That made sense. Charles wouldn't have left without a word. And besides, he was their chaperone: where they went, he had to go as well. "Well, good. So long as he's not going to abandon us . . ."

"I cannot imagine Charles abandoning you anywhere," Cecily murmured.

Rosalind's cheeks flushed. She kept her head down. The reaction was neither ladylike nor proper. She reminded herself again that she was here as her father's representative, and that this was the only reason Cecily and Charles were able to join her on her journey home in the first place. "I'm certain I don't know what you mean," she said, hiding a smile.

"Ohhhh, don't you?" Cecily teased. "Then I suppose I shan't say anything further about it." She paused. "Not in public, anyway. Now come along, I can't wait to see what sort of train goes beneath the sea."

As they lined up at the gate—still hidden by the massive curtain—the Kaiser delivered another harsh but triumphant-sounding line. Then he gave a sharp tug on a rope hanging near the podium. The curtain fell away. Even Rosalind had to gasp along with the crowd.

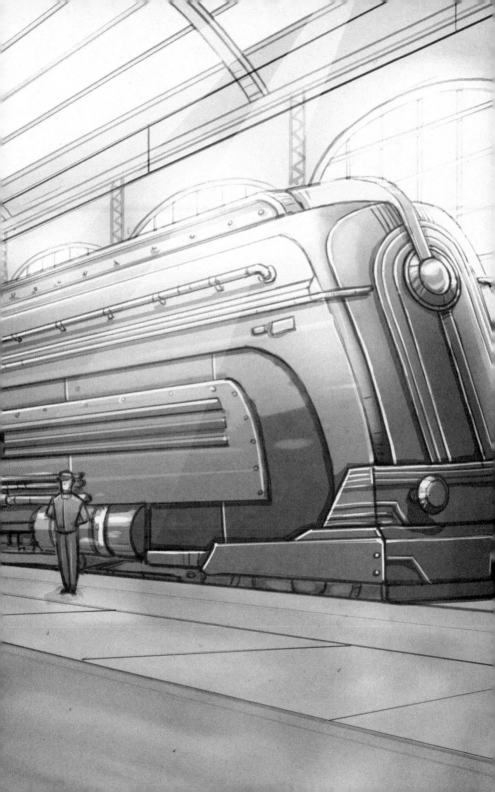

Switches Panel Resistance Blow-out Coil Line Line + Armature Overload Release Lug A touches Contact B when Switch is Closed + Field Resistance Line Low Voltage Release Pendant Switch Shunt Field Series Field Armature Ventilating Duct Pendant Switch Ventilating Holes Ventilating Air Intake

Chapter Three

Father has truly outdone himself. No wonder this is so important to him . . .

Rosalind's jaw hung slack. She had marveled at her father's creations before: the bridge over the Hudson River, the one now being constructed over Lake Michigan, his high-speed locomotives and luxurious two-story passenger cars. But the Transatlantic Express stretched along the platform for what seemed to be nearly half a mile. The carriages were far larger than normal as well—easily twice the width of a normal Pullman car, and almost twice as tall, with arched roofs—painted in beautiful blue and gold. The windows were round like portholes, cheekily mimicking the ships that the train sought to replace: a design quirk her father had insisted upon, no doubt. Above, rows of delicate wires spanned the whole length of the train, crackling and sparking with electricity.

"My word . . ." Rosalind murmured as she, Cecily, and Doris slowly made their way along the platform.

"It's like a ship!" Cecily clapped her hands together softly in excitement. "A ship on wheels! I simply adore it!"

"You must get one of your very own," Rosalind said wryly.

"I *must*. I'll be the talk of Mayfair."

"But wherever would you put it?" Rosalind asked. "It's very large and not likely to fit in the carriage house."

Cecily appeared to think about this for a moment. "Cornwall," she said, in all seriousness.

Rosalind sighed. Why Cecily still insisted in playing the flighty fool when they were alone—just the two of them—she could only imagine.

o o o

They entered the train far down the platform, beneath a great arched ceiling of glass and steel. The crowd was thankfully much smaller than the one in the concourse—only a hundred passengers were boarding—but with all the servants and porters, there were still more than enough people to make it slow going. Fortunately a small army of station attendants and conductors, all impeccably dressed in blue-and-gold uniforms, were on hand to keep things organized, issuing directions in a variety of languages.

"Here we go!" Cecily cried.

An attendant took her hand, helping her up the narrow carriage steps.

"Here we go," Rosalind echoed as the same man helped her aboard.

She couldn't help but squint back toward the station. There was still no sign of Charles and Harris. But how could she spot them in all the confusion? They'd just have to reconnect on the train.

Inside, the cars were beautifully adorned with polished wood, textured wallpaper, and intricately painted murals that lined the ceiling, depicting countless oceanic scenes—it was all so much more opulent than Father's American trains. Small electric lamps shaded with green glass lit the narrow corridor, which ran along the left-hand side of the sleeper cars. The hallway was only slightly wider than that of a normal railway carriage, and Rosalind found things a little cramped, what with the other passengers trying to find their compartments, and the porters moving baggage about the place. It seemed Father had been so intent on making the quarters as large and as grand as possible that he had forgotten that passengers also needed to be able to *access* them.

Typical of him, really: focusing on grandiosity while forgetting about little details like convenience.

Cecily suddenly made a noise of excitement. She began waving to a young woman about their age, who stood at the far end of the corridor. The girl was taller than Cecily, closer to Rosalind's height, with the porcelain-doll features and poise of the aristocracy—and with her slim dress and handbag, the fashion sense of a Parisian society girl.

"Alix! Alix!" Cecily cried.

The girl's face lit up. "Cecily?" she exclaimed.

"It's me!"

Cecily and the girl rushed toward each other, squealing in delight. They hugged each other tightly and exchanged kisses on both cheeks, giggling like schoolgirls. Rosalind watched the reunion with no idea what to say. Mostly she worried that this place was too claustrophobic for a meeting of old friends. A small traffic jam began to form behind them, and Rosalind gave the waiting passengers an apologetic smile.

"Cecily," she said, "I don't mean to interrupt, but . . ."

"Alix," Cecily purred to her friend, "you simply must meet Rose. Rosalind, this is my dear friend Alix von Hessen, of the Hessian von Hessens, you know."

Rosalind figured that there weren't too many von Hessens who *weren't* from Hesse, but making a joke now didn't seem polite.

"Wonderful to meet—" she began.

"She and I were at finishing school together," Cecily continued, talking over Rosalind with her usual exuberance. "In Switzerland, of course. All the best finishing schools are Swiss."

"Of course," Rosalind agreed, even though she had no clue.

"Yes, some of them," Alix said, her English polished and fluent, "though our old headmistress . . ."

"Ooooh, Madame Künzler . . . Kindly do not remind me." Cecily shuddered.

"I never knew you attended finishing school, Cecily," Rosalind said.

"Naturally," Cecily replied. "I insisted upon it. But look

at me now, being so rude. Alix, this is Rosalind Wallace. I call her Rose. I'm the only one who calls her that, but you may as well, isn't that right, Rose?"

Behind Rosalind, a porter coughed loudly.

"I . . . yes?" Rosalind's voice faltered.

Alix smiled and raised an eyebrow, as if to say, *Cecily's a handful, isn't she?* She extended a hand.

"It is very nice to meet you, Rosalind," she said. "If you are a friend of Cecily's, then I am certain we are going to get along wonderfully."

"She's my dearest friend in all the world," Cecily said. "And her father owns the railway. Isn't that fun?"

"The railway?" Alix asked. "You mean . . . *this* railway?" Her pale-blue eyes widened. "Oh, my. Then I am very pleased to meet you indeed, Miss Wallace."

Rosalind laughed, and then quickly remembered her manners. Smiling demurely, she nodded and said, "And I you, Miss von Hessen." Then a thought occurred to her. Cecily had given no title to accompany the name, but there were so many aristocrats traveling with them . . . "Or is it Lady von Hessen?" she asked, suddenly afraid that she had misspoken.

"Oh, why should any of us be so very formal?" Alix asked. "We are on a train that travels beneath the waves. Clearly all the rules of the world are being thrown to the wind."

"I suppose that's true," Rosalind agreed, grinning a little. She almost forgot the impatience of the other passengers. It was wonderful to hear an aristocrat speak so dismissively of protocol. London had been filled with aristocrats so obsessed with protocol that they practically fell all over themselves to observe it. They had been even worse than Rosalind's Old Money cousins in America. Yet here was Alix von Hessen, insisting that none of that mattered.

"And besides," Alix continued, her tone warm and genial, "if you are Cecily's dearest friend in all the world, I should like to think that we are already friends as well, Miss Wallace. Or . . . Rose? Yes?" She took Rosalind's hand.

Rosalind smiled. "I should like that very much, yes. And yes, you may call me Rose if you like. That will make two people. Things are so often better when they're shared."

"Then you must call me Alix."

"This is marvelous." Cecily beamed, then suddenly her face became very serious, peering down her nose at the grumbling passengers. "And now . . . let's see my stateroom."

"I think that would be best," Rosalind agreed quietly. "Before we're kicked off the train for causing a blockage."

"Don't be silly," chided Cecily. "They can't kick *you* off, can they? Your father would cancel the whole journey!"

❍   ❍   ❍

Cecily's compartment was by far the largest Rosalind had ever seen on one of her father's trains: it was a proper set of staterooms, rather than a cramped cabin. Just like on a ship. The floor was carpeted and the walls upholstered in matching green velvet. The brass adornments and fixtures on the walls were as brightly polished here as in the corridor, no doubt the work of diligent hands that had been working right up to boarding time. Father had truly spared no expense in this latest endeavor. She felt she should have known as much. But then, as she'd said herself, his business was his alone.

The furniture consisted of a wardrobe, a chest of drawers, and a table and chairs for entertaining visitors. There was even a writing desk by the round window. The bed was small by house standards, but for a train it was sizable, and it looked soft and warm, which were the best standards by which a bed could be judged. Cecily promptly threw all propriety to the wind and leapt upon it, cackling in delight as she bounced up and down.

"This is marvelous!" she cried.

"Now that you're settling in, Cecily, I think I'll be doing the same," Alix said, with another wry glance at Rosalind.

"Yes," Rosalind agreed absently. She walked in a circle around the room, examining the furnishings each in turn. She almost feared what would happen to the family if the Transatlantic Express wasn't a success. Father must have risked a fortune, no matter what Germany's investment had been. If the Transatlantic wasn't a success, they might suddenly become poor again, like Grandfather. Mother's family would never speak to them again; the only thing that kept them civil was the fact that Father's money allowed them to pay off Great-Uncle Horace's gambling debts.

All of which begged the question once again: Why

wasn't Father on the train keeping an eye on things? He had to be concerned. Or did he have that much faith in Rosalind? Had she underestimated him? Maybe he trusted her to be not only the family representative but also the business's watchdog.

"I've been thinking, there are so many things to do," Alix said in the silence. "I wonder if seven days is enough for it all. The dining room, the library, the tennis car, the concert hall . . ."

Cecily stopped bouncing and sat still, resting her chin on her hands. She looked at Rosalind. "Rose, why didn't you tell me they have a concert hall? You're supposed to keep me informed about these things."

Rosalind was hardly listening. Her eyes had fallen on a little brass tube beside the desk, mounted on the wall just next to the window. There was a sort of scoop-shaped tray at the bottom and a series of levers and dials that Rosalind could make neither heads nor tails of.

She glanced back at Cecily. "Cecily, I know nothing about the wonders aboard this train," she admitted. She turned to Alix. "How do you know about it?"

"I have *The Transatlantic Express Guide*," Alix replied, as if in on a secret. She produced a small printed brochure from her handbag and held it up. "It details every step of our journey and the amenities available onboard, and it even gives a list of respectable hotels to stay at in New York. I am very pleased by it."

Cecily groaned and flopped back on the bed. "Oooooh," she said. "Trust you to get excited about a piece of paper."

Alix rolled her eyes at Cecily's teasing. "I am very fond

of paper, in fact. And in much larger quantities. I read books, you see. In Switzerland, Cecily was always teasing me about it."

"That's something you two have in common," Cecily said, smirking at Rosalind from the bed. "You love books and I tease you about it."

"Incessantly," Rosalind confirmed. It was all well-intentioned, but it did wear on a person. She wondered if Alix felt the same way.

"There are far worse things to be teased over," Alix said.

"And more deserving ones," Rosalind added. She felt herself drawn to the strange pipe contraption next to the writing desk. "I wonder what this can be. Any ideas, Cecily?" It didn't seem right to ask Alix about it, having only just met the girl. One did not inquire about peculiar technological devices with new acquaintances unless they were male and much older and engineers by profession.

"I've no idea," Cecily said. "Could be a radiator. Or an ink dispenser."

"Oh, Cecily, you silly fool," Alix chided with a laugh. "It is a pneumatic tube, of course. For sending letters between cabins, I would think. Very clever of them to have thought of that."

"Huh," Rosalind said. She lifted the lid of the device, then let it fall shut again. "That rather makes sense." She had never seen a pneumatic postal device in person, but she had read about them. Alix was right: it *was* terribly clever. It was like having a telegraph for letters. It made good sense having one on the train, as it was both more private and more convenient than having one of the porters deliver a message.

Alix leaned past Rosalind, as carefully and politely as possible, then began fiddling with the dials and switches, muttering excitedly in German.

Rosalind glanced at Cecily for an explanation, but Cecily only raised an eyebrow and shrugged.

"Oh," Alix said, suddenly realizing her rudeness. She took a few steps back and resumed a dignified pose. "I do apologize, Miss Wallace. It is only that the machine is very complicated. It appears one can send messages directly to any cabin one chooses just by selecting the number. It might not even go to a central exchange first, which is very good for privacy. I am . . . I am impressed, and it has gotten the better of my manners. Do forgive me."

Alix sounded so earnest that Rosalind couldn't even think of being offended. She had never before heard another woman speak of gadgetry with such delight. It was much like when Aunt Mildred spoke of bicycling: peculiar, unladylike, but undeniably charming.

"There's nothing to forgive, Lady von Hessen," Rosalind said, grinning in spite of herself. "And I thought you were to call me Rose."

She sighed and smiled broadly in relief. "Yes, and you are to call me Alix. Commencing at once."

"Then you'll pardon me, Alix," Rosalind added, "because I should thank you. It's a fascinating device and thanks to you, I now know what the thing is. Left on my own, I feel certain I'd have mistaken it for a safe and stored my jewels in it, or something equally horrid."

Cecily swung her feet onto the floor, saying impatiently, "Yes, dear Alix is very technologically inclined, you know."

"I am not," Alix protested, blushing. "I simply . . . read books about things." She looked at Rosalind, perhaps for support.

"Oh, you needn't worry about Rose," Cecily said. "She's as bad as you are. She drives motorcars."

Alix's mouth went slack. Her eyes sparkled. "Is that so?"

Rosalind felt her cheeks getting hot. "I . . ." she began hesitantly. But then she steeled herself. Cecily had let the truth out, so there was no reason to deny it. Rosalind had already scandalized Society in America—not to mention London—with her illicit motoring. Why not scandalize Germany as well? "It's true," she said. "Whatever you may think of me for it, I am a motorist. And proudly so."

For good measure, she raised her chin and folded her arms. Let people say what they wished. Why should men have all the fun driving about in automobiles?

To her surprise, Alix clapped her hands together. "Cecily, your friend is simply wonderful. So spirited. Very . . . um . . . American." It sounded like a compliment, so Rosalind decided to take it as one. "Wherever did you find her?"

"Find me?" Rosalind said. Her arms fell to her side. The initial goodwill she'd felt toward Alix began to chafe. She'd heard similar "compliments" from friends of Cecily's in London; they spoke of her as if she weren't present, as if she were a lost puppy—or worse, a curiosity.

"Our fathers are old friends," Cecily explained. "And

a good thing, too. You must meet her father sometime, Alix. You really must. He's as peculiar as she is." Then she whispered rather loudly, "He's the one who gave her the motorcar."

"I *can* hear you, you know," Rosalind grumbled.

"Oh, don't be cross, Rose," Cecily said with a giggle. "Don't mind us and what we say. We certainly don't mean anything ill by it. Do we, Alix?"

Alix quickly shook her head. "No, no, not at all. I do apologize, Rose; I meant no offense. Cecily and I are just happy to see each other."

Cecily fell back onto the bed, arms spread wide as she stared up at the ceiling. "I should like to be a motorist one day. It must be sooo exciting. Whizzing through the countryside at twenty miles an hour!"

Best not to dwell on their aristocratic prejudices, Rosalind decided. They couldn't help it. They were like Father that way; he'd developed his own airs after he'd made his fortune. He'd become one of them. No, it was better to play along. She beckoned them both to lean in conspiratorially and stage-whispered, "I've driven over thirty, actually."

"You never!" Cecily exclaimed. "That's faster than a horse." She covered her mouth as if she had just heard something wonderfully scandalous—which, to be fair, she had. "You're such an eccentric, Rose. You and Alix both, what with your machines and motorcars and things . . ."

"You are one to talk, Cecily," Alix said. "You are as bad as we two, and do not pretend otherwise. You and your love of clocks . . ."

Cecily's eyes flashed to Rosalind. Her face turned red.

She grabbed one of the feather pillows and flung it at Alix, who evaded it by scampering to one side. "You promised you wouldn't tell a soul."

"Clocks?" Rosalind repeated, baffled.

"Oh, yes," Alix replied, nodding a few times. "She is clock-mad, our Cecily. She builds them, you know. Big ones, little ones, watches even."

Cecily grabbed another pillow to hide behind. "Lies! All of it!" she cried, but Rosalind knew Cecily well enough to tell when her friend was putting on an act, gleeful at being indignant—which was most of the time.

"In Switzerland we shared rooms," Alix told Rosalind. "Day and night it was all *tick-tock, tick-tock*."

A realization struck her. "So that's why you have so many clocks in the parlor," Rosalind said. "I thought they belonged to Charles."

"Belonged to Charles?" Cecily's smile vanished. "Hardly. My poor old brother knows nothing about assembling clocks. Doesn't understand the first thing about it, I tell you. Far too busy mucking about with his guns and shooting and tweed. Ohhh, tweed. Dreadful fabric. Simply dreadful."

Having seen Charles wearing tweed during a recent excursion to the country, Rosalind was inclined to disagree. But best to keep that to herself, too.

"Speaking of Charles . . ." she ventured, then paused, uncertain of how to ask after him without sounding improper. "Shouldn't we find him?"

"Charles is *here*?" Alix asked Cecily

"Um . . ." Cecily said, suddenly at a loss for words.

"Well . . . Well, no. Obviously not with us here now. I mean, that is to say . . ."

"He accompanied us all the way from England," Rosalind chimed in, wondering at Cecily's odd behavior. Perhaps the siblings had gotten into an argument she hadn't been aware of. She pushed the thought from her mind; it was none of her business. "And then we lost him in the crowd at the station. He must be onboard somewhere. He's traveling to New York with us." She hesitated, then added, "He's our chaperone."

"Yes, but only as far as my parents are concerned," Cecily said, collecting herself. "Charles is clearly being Charles. Who really understands anything that he does?" She hopped out of bed. "Now then, let's not talk any more about my silly brother. Such a dull subject."

Alix glanced at Rosalind and shrugged.

"I know what we should do," Cecily said, taking Rosalind's arm. "We should go along to the restaurant car and have some lemonade. Doesn't that sound like fun?"

"Yes, but . . ." Alix appeared puzzled at first, and then she smiled. "That is a wonderful idea. I could do with some refreshment before I get settled."

Before Rosalind knew what was happening, Alix had taken her by the other arm and the two girls were guiding her toward the door.

"But, Cecily," Rosalind protested. "What about Charles? Don't you think we should make an effort to find him?"

Cecily groaned. "Rose, my dearest, you mustn't insist on discussing my brother so. People will talk."

Clearly, there *was* something going on between the siblings—Cecily was never this mean-spirited or rude—but arguing about it wouldn't make Cecily any more inclined to explain herself. It was best to put her at ease and in charge; that was always the trick for getting Cecily to reveal something she was trying to hide.

"You're right, Cecily," she said. "Your brother can look after himself."

"Very sensible, Rose." Cecily gave her arm a gentle squeeze. "And after all, lemonade is far more important than boys."

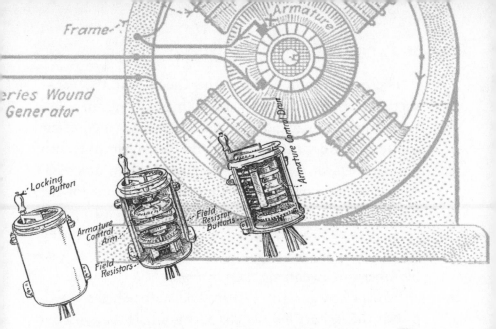

Frame

ries Wound
Generator

Locking
Button

Armature
Control
Arm

Field
Resistors

Field
Resistor
Buttons

Armature Control Dial

Armature

There were three dining cars in First Class. The tables were circular and covered with woven tablecloths of blue and gold—the same colors as practically everything else on the train. That, too, was typical of Father: throwing gold all over the place like King Midas. Yet here again he'd reached for new heights. The china and silver were all sparkling, brand-new. Ornate crystal chandeliers hung very close to the ceiling, presumably to avoid striking anyone in the head.

An attendant seated them at one of the tables near a round window. Within minutes, Rosalind found herself relaxing, sipping lemonade with Cecily and her new friend, Alix. She glanced outside; the platform was nearly empty. The people outside had presumably all either boarded the train or been shooed away by the station attendants. They would be leaving soon.

48 G.D. Falksen

There were only a few other people in the car—
everyone else was probably unpacking. Among these few
were some German and Austrian aristocrats, though she
spotted one Russian in military uniform. A pair of French
businessmen sat at a nearby table, speaking in quiet and
serious tones about the train and what it meant for the
future of Europe. Rosalind was tempted to eavesdrop. She
could almost hear Father's voice in her head, lecturing
these two about the unstoppable march of progress. Led
by American machinery. Led by *him*.

Perhaps he was right. Perhaps Old Europe had a reason
to fear the upstart industrialists, not only in America but
also inside their own borders. Entrepreneurs who made
their own fortunes did pose a risk to the old order. And
this was a good thing, the *best* thing. The collapse of class
barriers, the breakup of empires . . . But Father was so
blind in so many ways. Particularly when it came to his
own daughter. Women played no part in shaping his ver-
sion of a new and better future.

Rosalind tore herself away from the whispering
Frenchmen. Cecily was her usual talkative self, prattling
on about the drapery and the glassware, plainly making
every effort to avoid the topic of Charles. Before Rosalind
could ask after him again, Alix smiled at her.

"Tell me, Rosalind, what is it like to drive a motorcar?"
she asked.

"Oh, it is very exciting," Rosalind answered. "Like
riding a horse while sitting in a chair. The wind rushes
against your face."

Alix nodded and sipped her lemonade. "That sounds

wonderful. I should very much like to drive a motorcar one day."

"When we arrive in America, I will take you for a ride in Father's," Rosalind said, and she meant it.

"Won't he mind?" Cecily asked.

"I doubt he'll even notice," Rosalind answered. She bit her lip, realizing what she had just said. But it was true, and it spoke to exactly what she'd been thinking a moment ago: Father rarely paid much attention to anything she did, except when it served his own interests.

Alix set her drink down. "This voyage shall be great fun, I know it. My goodness, Rosalind, it must be very exciting to be the daughter of an American engineer who builds such incredible trains—"

"He does more than just build trains, silly," Cecily interrupted. "He builds bridges and tunnels and things, too." She looked at Rosalind. "He must be very clever with numbers."

"With mathematics, yes . . ." Rosalind answered. "And you know, he always said I took after him in that." She glanced at Alix. "There was many a summer when Father had me doing the ledgers for the company, to make sure it was all in order. He said I was very good at it." *But of course*, she added silently, *it was all about helping him, not about my own abilities.*

"Your father made you his accountant?" Alix whispered. "That is . . . I suppose I cannot even imagine it. How exciting."

Rosalind attempted to smile, not even sure why she'd brought it up. At the time she'd felt that she and Father had something in common, binding them together. But her smile fell as she remembered again what Father always said to her when she'd finished: "If only you had been born my son." Spoken every time like it was a compliment.

"Rosalind, is something the matter?" Alix asked.

She put the thoughts of her father from her mind and quickly said, "No, no, nothing at all."

Cecily threw up her hands. "Alix, darling, you *must* stop pestering Rose about such silly things. You're embarrassing her. She loves books and writing and she's a machinist. She's even piloted submersibles. There: now we know everything about my American friend's sordid past. There are much more important things to discuss, like which hat I should wear to dinner. Because *truly*, if I wear the red silk—"

"Submersibles?" Alix interrupted. "Cecily can't be telling the truth, can she? Is that true, Rose?"

"*Once*," Rosalind replied to Alix. Because *truly*: she, too, would rather discuss Cecily's choice of hat. To Cecily she said, more forcefully, "Once. My father insisted I accompany him when he tested rescue boats for the railway . . ."

Cecily grinned and sipped her drink.

"I think it sounds very exciting," Alix said. "And dangerous. Were you not afraid of drowning?"

With a glare at Cecily, Rosalind replied, "Of course I was." Her voice rose. "Sitting in a metal box under New York Harbor? Wouldn't you be afraid?" She bit her lip and turned back toward the window. "Perhaps drowning isn't the best topic of conversation."

"Oh, I don't mind," Cecily said impishly. "I enjoy a bit of a thrill. And I'm a very good swimmer."

o o o

Soon they were off. There was a small jolt, barely perceptible, and then bright sunshine as they steamed out of Hamburg and across the German countryside. Before long the tracks began sloping downward into the earth. Less than an hour after their departure, a tunnel closed over them. The train was already underground, and still there was no sign of Charles. Rosalind realized her palms were clammy. He was their chaperone. He should have come looking for them. He should have easily found them by now.

"Cecily," she said, "shouldn't we go looking for Charles and make certain he's aboard? I'm worried he may have missed the train for some reason. Perhaps he was waylaid back at the station—"

"Don't be absurd, Rose," Cecily interrupted. "Charles can look after himself. It's not my sisterly duty to play nursemaid to him."

"But Cecily, he's our chaperone."

"Now isn't that peculiar?" Cecily remarked.

Alix nodded and stood up from the table, their lemonades long finished. "It is peculiar. I will say, this is the first time my parents have allowed me to travel by myself . . ."

"No, not that," Cecily groaned. "The tunnel is peculiar. I'd have thought we would be under the water by now. I was looking forward to seeing fish. Don't tell me the tunnel goes underground the entire way?"

Rosalind laughed in spite of her worry. *Besides,* she thought, *he must be onboard. This is a huge train. He could be anywhere.* "The ocean is a bit too deep for that. No, the train goes underwater when we reach the coast. It's very difficult to support the weight of a train in the water, you see." She began gesturing with her hands. Her mother always called this a horrible habit. But Mother said that about a lot of things, so Rosalind paid little mind to her admonitions. "And there are these buoys all the way along the tunnel to keep us afloat."

"Buoys?" Cecily asked, gazing into the window at her own reflection.

"Yes, but you see, when the train comes through, it changes the weight of the tunnel by tons," Rosalind continued. She was actually excited at the prospect of Cecily's fascination with something mechanical. If Cecily secretly enjoyed tinkering with clocks, perhaps she really did have interests beyond deciding on the right hat for the evening. Maybe it was even a good thing Charles hadn't found them yet. Cecily might open up if there weren't any men or boys around.

But then she stopped herself. Cecily and Alix were both staring blankly at her, doing their best to be polite.

"It's not really all that interesting, I suppose," Rosalind said.

Cecily patted Rosalind on the arm. "Oh, don't be silly, Rose, it's utterly fascinating. Just like that time when you told me all about ballooning."

Rosalind suppressed a scowl. Cecily was lying; this was Cecily's polite way of telling her she was being boring.

Alix, still standing, removed her brochure from her handbag. "I do not mean to interrupt, but I believe we should visit the arboreal car before we adjourn to our staterooms to change for the evening."

"Arboreal car? They have an arboreal car?" Cecily paused. "What's an arboreal car?"

"It's an indoor park," Rosalind explained. "Trees and flowers and shrubbery, that sort of thing. And the lights make it look like it's the correct time of day, or so I was told."

"Oooh," Cecily replied. She stood and peered at the brochure over Alix's shoulder. "It has a rose garden."

"Yes, I know," Rosalind murmured.

"We simply must see it before it is overrun by the teeming masses."

"Cecily," Rosalind said softly, "I know that you would like to go exploring, but we really ought to ask a porter to help us find Charles. At the very least we should ask for his room number, so we can send him a message telling him we're here. He must be worried to distraction about you."

"Don't be absurd," Cecily told her. "Charles doesn't worry about anything."

"He worries about *you*," Rosalind said, ever more certain that the siblings had had some sort of argument at the station. But then again, Rosalind hadn't seen any such argument . . .

"They have a library!" Alix announced.

"Oh, Alix," Cecily said, "you sound just like Rose." She looked at Rosalind and teased, "You've only just met her and already you're a bad influence."

Rosalind remained silent. Cecily insisted on being evasive? Fine. If the de Veres were having an argument, they would avoid each other for a little while, then they would make up and all would be back to normal. Rosalind had seen it happen before. Perhaps he was avoiding *them* as well. The best thing to do, Rosalind concluded, was to explore First Class as thoroughly as possible in the hopes of crossing paths with him.

"You know, Cecily," she said, "you are absolutely right. We *should* explore. We should take advantage of this wondrous train."

Cecily grinned. She raised her finger into the air and exclaimed, "Marvelous. To the rose garden!"

Rosalind exchanged a glance with Alix. They nodded to each other. Then they both looked at Cecily.

"To the library," they replied in unison.

o   o   o

Rosalind had seen the "libraries" on some of her father's other trains—small, stuffy rooms packed with a tiny collection of crumbling books nobody wanted to read. This library was the size of an entire car, with a fine selection of books and several comfortable chairs to read in. It was at the rear of the First Class section of the train, rather near to the arboreal car, as luck would have it.

Along the way, they passed back through the sleeper cars, with Rosalind keeping a wary eye out for Charles the entire time. Car after car after car . . . A First Class fraction of one hundred passengers did not seem like a great number—certainly not when compared with the number typically onboard a ship—but on a train it appeared to demand an endless amount of space.

And beyond the sleeper cars were various amenities: parlors, an art gallery, a concert hall (where a pianist played at all times), and of course a smoking room, open only to men. (They could have it, though; Rosalind hated the smell of tobacco.) At every open door, she peeked in and made a quick search for Charles, and every time she was disappointed.

The library car was quiet and dark and lined floor-to-ceiling with bookshelves. There were high-backed armchairs and a couple of tables for reading, although the librarian on duty had a ledger on his desk: passengers could sign out books. Again, there was no Charles, but Rosalind had not given up hope. She took a moment to examine the titles on the nearest shelf . . . mostly novels and books of poetry, but some nonfiction as well.

Cecily tugged on Rosalind's hand. "Come along," she urged impatiently. "The flowers are waiting."

And Charles, too, I hope, Rosalind thought. Her heart fluttered. Her palms felt clammy again. The arboreal car was at the very back of First Class, and the last car on the train that was accessible only to First Class passengers. Unless Charles was hidden away in his stateroom, he was there. He had to be.

"Very well, let's be quick about it," Rosalind said.

Once they'd emerged from the dim silence of the library, however, she wanted to linger. This was the train's crowning jewel. It was no accident that the arboreal car was at the very rear of First Class. She had seen her father's sketches for it some years ago, and even some more recent photographs of it. But the sight in person was quite beyond what she had expected . . . especially the massive ceiling of arched glass, through which shone what appeared to be sunlight: the work of powerful hidden lamps.

Whereas the corridors and dining cars were decked in blue and gold, and the library a typical burgundy and brown, the arboreal car was awash in green. A few small paths wove their way past bushes, trees, and marble planters filled with flowers. Rosalind almost forgot she was onboard a moving train. If it weren't for the gentle rattling on the tracks, she could have been in a greenhouse or a well-tended park.

Cecily squealed with laughter, swept up in the wonder of it all. She grabbed hands with Rosalind and Alix and dragged them down one of the paths. At each turn, Rosalind kept her eyes open for Charles, but there was no sign of him. So he had to be in his compartment—but only Cecily could inquire about its location. Unmarried young women didn't go about asking after men who weren't relatives.

"Isn't it marvelous?" Cecily said, twirling in a circle. She stopped in place and raised her hands. "A garden on a train. Who could have imagined?"

"Rosalind's father, I should think," Alix said with a smile as she looked around. "But yes, it is quite beautiful."

"I do hope it becomes something of a trend," Cecily said. "What do you think, Rose?"

"The air's certainly fresher," Rosalind said. Though

now that she had some time to reflect, she wondered if Father's imagination hadn't actually gotten the better of him. Potted ferns were one thing, but a whole miniature forest was simply too surreal for her comfort. Gardens were gardens and trains were trains, and the two were not meant to be crammed one inside the other. But it was rather pretty.

"I don't know if I like it or if I don't," she concluded.

"You do," Cecily clarified for her. "You simply don't know it yet."

Rosalind turned to her. "Perhaps I do, but we can come back. Right now I think the two of us should find a porter and ask—"

A high-pitched whistle silenced her in midsentence. It rippled through the air, so loud and sharp that she nearly jumped. She exchanged frightened looks with Cecily and Alix.

"What was that?" Alix asked.

The whistle sounded again—this time only a short burst, thankfully. A gravelly and slightly distorted voice boomed from the gilded grillwork near the ceiling, first in German. A welcome announcement, Rosalind realized, and the three of them relaxed. A moment later, the voice repeated itself in accented English.

"Good evening, ladies and gentlemen. This is your captain speaking. It is my great honor to welcome you aboard the Transatlantic Express for this, our maiden voyage."

"My goodness," Alix whispered. "The captain speaking to us? How very exciting!"

Cecily craned her head from side to side as she looked up at the ceiling. "I wonder how it's done," she mused.

"It could be a voice pipe," Alix offered. "I have seen them on ships."

Rosalind shook her head. "No, the sound would never carry the whole length." She pursed her lips for a moment and thought about the matter. Then it came to her. "It must be something electrical. Perhaps a telephone, with an amplified receiver."

Cecily's eyes widened. "I didn't know they could do such a thing!"

Above them, the captain's voice continued to blare: "I hope you have settled in comfortably. We are approaching the coast. If you would care to look out of the nearest window, you will be treated to a sight seen only by a handful of people in all the world."

Rosalind caught a shape moving behind the fronds near the door to the Second Class carriages. Curious, she turned to get a better look and saw what she thought to be a shadow lurking behind a tree, the shadow of someone watching them. Was it Charles after all?

She took a step nearer and saw one of the porters adjusting a flowerpot. No, not him. Then, as Rosalind turned away, she saw someone in a brown suit disappear behind one of the bushes. For a moment, she was reminded of the stranger at the station, gazing at them from the crowd. But was it the same man? After all, many people wore brown suits. Still, it was the same shade and pattern . . . But so what? He was a passenger, enjoying the wonders of this car, as well he should.

"We're about to go underwater!" Cecily shouted frantically. "There are no windows in this place! Quickly! Quickly! Someone find a window!"

Rosalind glanced back toward Second Class. The porter was still busy; the man in the suit was gone. "Let's go back to the library," she urged calmly. "There are plenty of windows there." She peered around for Alix, but the girl had wandered off into the flora.

"Alix will catch up with us," Cecily said, tugging Rosalind after her.

Passengers were already huddled around the circular panes of glass, murmuring to one another about what they were about to see and whether it would really be worth leaving the most comfortable chair in the library just to see it. Rosalind and Cecily hurried to an unoccupied window and waited.

For about half a minute, the glass remained dark. Rosalind was given to wonder if it had really been such a good idea to rush in for a look. They had surely looked silly, but then so had everyone else . . .

In that instant, the blackness beyond the window vanished into a thick haze of deep blue-green.

She and Cecily drew in a breath at the same time. It was as if someone had splashed paint over the glass. Only it was water: the cold, swirling water of the North Sea, and they were inside it.

Rosalind leaned forward and stared, transfixed, as fish darted past them—almost too fast even to register, but close enough to touch if not for the two glass barriers that separated them. Rosalind felt giddy. *We are beneath the sea.*

Until that moment, she hadn't appreciated the full measure of what that meant.

"Gosh, that's a great deal of water," Cecily whispered.

Rosalind smiled. Seeing Cecily at a loss for words, genuinely, was almost as remarkable as the view.

The door at the rear of the car opened, and Alix hurried in to join them. For a second or two, she almost seemed disinterested, as if being underwater were a common experience for her. But as she stared out the window, she began to tremble. Suddenly her eyes bulged and her jaw dropped.

"My God," she said to Rosalind, "that is the ocean?"

"'Tis indeed," Rosalind replied.

"But . . . But . . ." Alix stammered. "But the tunnel. It is glass. It will break. We will drown!"

Rosalind blinked at Alix. The girl's skin had turned from porcelain to bone white. She took Alix's hand and tried to calm her. Having grown up with her father, Rosalind preferred to approach this adventure with the same attitude she had toward flying in a zeppelin: best to be amazed by the view without acknowledging the terror of it. Still, she was troubled at just how extreme Alix's reaction was: first disinterest, then panic. But who was Rosalind to judge someone she had only just met? No doubt the girl had led a sheltered life thus far.

"Don't be afraid," she soothed. "We're perfectly safe. Do you think my father would risk his own daughter's life?" Then she added, jokingly and conspiratorially, "I'll tell you a secret: I think he's more concerned that if something dreadful happens to us, it will start another pan-European war. And that would be bad for business."

Alix managed a shaky laugh. "Yes, I suppose they wouldn't risk such a thing if they did not have faith in the machine. Or the tunnel." She squeezed Rosalind's hand, perhaps without even realizing it. "But . . . it is glass. The tunnel is glass. What will stop it from breaking?"

"It was specially made just for this purpose, so it's more durable than normal glass," Rosalind said. "And it's half a foot thick, so it's not particularly prone to breaking. But it's unbreakable, anyway, according to my father. Something to do with chemistry. I don't really know the details."

Of course, Father had told her those details at great length, but she hadn't paid much attention. Chemistry was so very dull. You couldn't tinker with chemicals the way you could with an engine or a bicycle.

Alix took a small step back from the window. "Oh, I do not think I can stand to watch the sea any longer," she said. "It gives me chills. Come along, let us go to my compartment. Cecily, I have so many new dresses to show you . . ."

"Wonderful!" Cecily cried. "I shall help you decide what to wear for dinner tonight."

"Quite wonderful, yes," Rosalind said shortly. She let go of Alix and took Cecily by the hand, looking her in the eye. "Cecily, before we do that, you and I must find a member of the train staff and inquire about Charles. We have been from tip to toe of First Class, and he is nowhere."

"Yes, but . . ." Cecily stammered, squirming as she no doubt tried to dream up some new excuse.

"I do not know what has passed between you and Charles, but we need to find him before the night is over," Rosalind stated. "I need you to ask a conductor, as his sister, for the number of his compartment. And then we can all return to having fun, all right?"

"She is right, Cecily," Alix said softly.

Cecily glared at her.

Alix shrugged. "Tell us. Where is your brother? What is he doing? It is . . . strange."

For a moment Rosalind thought that Cecily was going to argue with them, or try to evade the question again, but instead she put on a serious face and nodded.

"You are quite right, both of you," she said. "I have allowed my amusement to get the better of me, when I should have been more sensible. When we go to dress for dinner, I will find a conductor and ask after Charles. He'll certainly be in his room getting ready at that time. And I will bring him along to dinner, and it will all be wonderful."

Rosalind sighed. "Thank you, Cecily. That's all I ask."

"But first," Cecily added with a smirk, "we simply must go with Alix and help her choose something to wear for dinner. Just think, Rose: new dresses. They're your favorite things, aren't they? After books and bicycles and trains, that is."

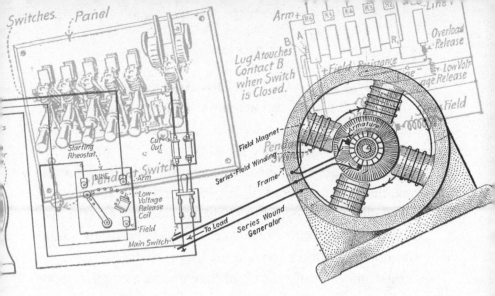

Rosalind was well aware of how miraculous this evening was. She was having dinner beneath the English Channel. A fine dinner, at that. She was doing something nobody else in history except those aboard this train, aboard these very dining cars, had done. She should have been savoring the miracle. Or at least savoring the food. But enjoyment was impossible.

Not only was Charles still absent; so was Cecily.

Everyone else from First Class had long since crowded into the cars, including Alix. Not wanting to be the last ones milling around, she and Rosalind sat at the one remaining table, set for five. A steward came to take their orders, and still no Cecily. It was only when Rosalind's roast chicken arrived that Cecily arrived, too. She swept into the room and made a beeline for the table, her smile bright but her expression uncertain.

Chapter Five

"Cecily, where is Charles?" Rosalind demanded.

"Um . . ." Cecily sat, her smile faltering. "Well, that's the funny thing."

"But where *is* he?" Alix added.

"The . . . um . . . The conductor told me that Charles gave the crew a note to be left in my room," Cecily said. She avoided their eyes but spoke confidently, careful not to stumble any more over her words. "But there was a mix-up and it didn't arrive until I went to dress."

Rosalind suddenly felt the chill of unease along her back.

"Apparently Charles isn't coming," Cecily finished.

"To dinner?" Alix asked. "Why not?"

"He's not on the train," Cecily clarified, still trying to appear cheerful. Her eyes eventually settled on Alix.

Rosalind's heart began to thump. This was her worst fear, confirmed. *"What?"* she asked in as soft a tone as she could manage.

Cecily took a drink of water. "Apparently he was called away at the station by telegram. From Father. Something of vital importance. Business. Defense of the Realm. Whitehall. That sort of thing."

"'That sort of thing?'" Rosalind repeated in disbelief.

"Cecily, this is terrible," Alix whispered.

"He said we're to have a wonderful time and that he'll join us in New York as soon as possible," Cecily added, as if that made everything better.

Rosalind shook her head, breathing deeply in an effort to keep calm. She was used to fighting moments of panic, especially onboard trains. But this was different. This panic had nothing to do with the train itself.

"Cecily, listen to me," she said, "whatever Charles told you in that letter can't be true. Your father did not summon him away. Not without telling you. Charles was supposed to travel with us to America. He's supposed to be chaperoning us. It's the only reason your parents allowed you to come with me! And I am certain they would have notified my father as well, if my chaperone hadn't boarded."

Cecily frowned. "Is that what's troubling you?"

"Yes, it is," Rosalind said between clenched teeth, leaning forward to emphasize her point. "You are sixteen years old."

"And you're seventeen," Cecily countered, though she gave no indication as to why this was important.

"Yes, and we are both unmarried," Rosalind said. Her eyes flashed to Alix, who looked equally bewildered as to why Cecily was being so thick about the matter. Cecily was usually the first person to comment on social propriety. "Your brother was supposed to supervise you—well, us." She quickly caught herself before the peculiarities of the situation misled her. "Cecily, think about your reputation."

Cecily scoffed. "Since when have you cared for reputation?"

"Not mine," Rosalind snapped. "Yours."

"Cecily, that is not very nice," Alix said tersely. "I am certain that Rosalind cares very much about her reputation."

While it was kind of Alix to rush to her defense, Rosalind felt that it was only right to reward the girl's kindness with honesty. "I appreciate it, but I don't, actually," she said. "Well, I mean, within reason. I drive motorcars and I'm a suffragist, so my reputation is already a bit uncertain." She forced an awkward smile.

Rosalind hadn't intended on mentioning her private

suffragist convictions—not to a near stranger, and not on this voyage at all—but then she hadn't imagined she'd be traveling unchaperoned, either. Now the cat was out of the bag, and it stood to reason that Alix might think ill of her for it. Driving a motorcar for fun was one thing; insisting upon the right to vote was quite another.

Alix blinked a few times. "Suffragist?" she asked. She sounded momentarily confused. "Ah. You mean . . . votes for women, yes?"

"Yes, votes for women," Rosalind said, nodding. "And in general."

"Dear Rose is dreadfully anti-imperial," Cecily explained. She spoke as if this were just another peculiar eccentricity, like driving motorcars.

"Anti-imperial?" Alix asked, sounding even more confused.

Rosalind knew that Cecily was bringing up the point to distract her, but it was a topic that Rosalind took seriously enough to oblige. Besides, she was furious with her friend, furious with her friend's brother, too. Cecily de Vere could use a good dose of anti-imperialism right now.

"I just think that the Indians ought to decide who rules India, for example. The Irish, Ireland. The Congolese, the Congo. Et cetera." She paused for a moment, trying very hard not to launch into a tirade. *Don't do it*, she told herself. *Not in front of someone you've only just met* . . . But dash it all, she was mad, and there was a principle at stake. "Think about this," she said to Cecily. "How would you feel if the French invaded England and turned *it* into a colony? Not very happy, I suspect."

Cecily grinned, clearly pleased Rosalind had taken the

bait. She turned to Alix. "Meet my dear friend Rosalind, the crusader. Isn't she just wonderful?"

Alix was staring at Rosalind, a smile playing on her lips. It was not quite the horrified look Rosalind had anticipated. Was she amused? Rosalind felt her face turning red with embarrassment. It was easy enough to stand fast against hostility; amusement was altogether a harder thing to combat. She fixed her gaze on Cecily.

"And don't think that you have distracted me from the original point," she snapped, which only made Cecily giggle. "No, I am serious about this. Where is Charles? He was supposed to accompany us."

Cecily grinned wickedly and leaned toward Alix. "Ever since we got on the train, it's been all 'Charles this' and 'Charles that.' I rather suspect Rose has taken a bit of a fancy to my brother."

Rosalind's cheeks were burning now. She knew that Cecily wasn't being intentionally cruel, but still it was horrid of her to make light of something so personal. Not that it was even true. Yes, Charles was very handsome and very charming, but he had never given her any indication of interest. She wasn't even certain of her own feelings, and they'd certainly never spoken about it . . .

Alix and Cecily suddenly sat up straight.

A shadow fell across the table. Rosalind looked up to see a pair of young men standing over them. One wore evening dress: a tailcoat and white tie; the other wore an officer's uniform colored a deep blue, with brightly polished buttons. Both were bright-eyed and cleanly shaven. Both were more than a little handsome. Rosalind glanced back at Cecily and Alix.

"Good evening, gentlemen," Cecily said wryly, addressing the young men like a queen entertaining petitioners. "I do hope that you speak English, for that is the only language that we use at this table."

The two fellows looked at each other and chuckled a little, very clearly entertained. The one in uniform bowed his head politely and answered, with a pronounced German accent, "We do, yes, Fräulein. And please forgive our intrusion."

"You are forgiven," Cecily decreed. She looked from Alix to Rosalind for confirmation. "Yes?"

"Yes," Rosalind and Alix said, almost together.

"Allow me to introduce myself," the officer said. "I am Lieutenant Jacob Hoffmeyer of the Prussian Army. And my friend—"

"Erich Steiner, at your service," the other finished, bowing in turn.

"We are both at your service," Jacob added.

Rosalind raised an eyebrow. Cecily and Alix smiled demurely.

"Well met, Lieutenant Hoffmeyer, Herr Steiner," Cecily said, again the regal and composed queen of the dinner table. She tilted her head slightly toward each of them in turn. "I am Lady Cecily de Vere. Of the Exham de Veres. No doubt you have heard of us?"

"Oh, well, I . . ." Jacob stammered.

"Of course we have," Erich interjected. "The Exham de Veres, one of the noblest families in all of England. Why, just this morning Jacob remarked to me how wonderful it would be to meet an Exham de Vere."

"I did?" Jacob asked. There was a moment's pause. "Ah, yes, I did. Just this morning. I recall it distinctly. Yes."

Rosalind almost laughed. So Jacob was not as well schooled in subtlety and charm as his friend Erich. It was rather endearing.

Cecily motioned to Alix and said, "And this is my traveling companion, Lady Alix von Hessen. Of the Hessian von Hessens."

Alix's face looked momentarily pained. She recovered with a smile. Erich coughed to hide a laugh. Jacob simply appeared to be bewildered at Cecily's very redundant statement. Rosalind couldn't blame him.

"I would imagine so," Erich said. Then he bowed his head and said, "An honor, Lady von Hessen."

"And also a pleasure, I hope," Alix said lightly.

"Oh, yes, of course," Jacob said, blushing a little. "Very much a pleasure."

"And finally, Miss Rosalind Wallace," Cecily announced. "Our chaperone."

Rosalind glared daggers at Cecily before turning to the two young men. "No, no, I'm not the chaperone—"

"Yes, she is," Cecily insisted.

Let it go, Rosalind thought. Now was not the time to get into an argument with Cecily. No, it was best to play along, to have some fun—for now. "My friends call me what they will," Rosalind said breezily. "I have no control over them. Gentlemen, it is a pleasure to meet you both. To what do we owe the honor?"

Erich laughed clumsily. Jacob bowed his head again.

"We were instructed by the head steward to join you at

your table," Erich explained. "There are no other places in any of the cars."

"We do not wish to intrude," Jacob added. "Only we are a little hungry . . ."

Cecily pretended to be horrified. "You should have said so at the outset. For goodness' sake, sit down at once. Now, where is a waiter . . . ?" She began snapping her fingers to draw the attention of the staff.

Both Erich and Jacob looked relieved at the invitation and sat, Jacob next to Alix, Erich next to Rosalind. Rosalind found herself smiling at Erich. For a moment, she felt a little awkward. But then again, why shouldn't she smile? They had just met. It was the polite thing to do. And yes, he was rather handsome; even more so when he returned her smile with one of his own.

Stop it, she told herself. *He's just being polite, and you've only just met him. Don't be foolish.*

The seconds wore on. She opened her mouth to speak but found it was dry. His eyes hadn't left hers. "I recommend the chicken," she said. It was the only thing she could think of to say.

"What . . . ?" Erich asked, blinking in surprise. He looked down at her plate and laughed. "Oh, I see. Yes, good, good. I will have the chicken, then."

"Well . . . I mean . . ." Rosalind said, stumbling a little. "You don't need to, I just thought I should recommend it."

"But it sounds like a very good recommendation," Erich said.

Suddenly the awkward silence returned. What was more, she felt the rest of the eyes at the table focused on her. This time she did not let the silence linger. Instead, she turned to Jacob and said, "Lieutenant Hoffmeyer, you are in the army?"

"Yes," Jacob said proudly. "Artillery."

"Oooh," Cecily interjected. "That sounds very . . . dangerous?"

Jacob shrugged. "I do not know about it being dangerous. I . . . have not seen combat yet. Nor, I suppose, do I expect to anytime soon. It has been so long since the last war, thank God."

Before he could go on, the door to the dining car flew open. A man burst in, nearly colliding with one of the stewards. He was middle-aged, paunchy, with graying hair that almost matched the color of his drab suit. He stormed the length of the room toward the front of the train, snapping in German for the waitstaff to get out of his way. For a moment, all conversation in the dining car halted. In the silence, another man—younger and fleeter, also dressed in a drab suit—raced after him.

When both had gone, Rosalind exchanged a puzzled glance with the boys. Jacob leaned in across the table and asked in amazement, "You do know who that was, yes? The fat one?"

"No," Rosalind answered. "Who?"

"Inspector Bauer," he said.

"Who?" Erich asked.

"That's what I would like to know," Cecily said. "Imagine! Interrupting our dinner like that."

"He's the man in charge of security on the train," Jacob explained. "There is a picture of him in the brochure,

along with the captain and the head steward." He quickly
patted his uniform. "I cannot remember if I brought my
copy with me . . ."

Erich laughed, trying to lighten the mood. "Jacob,
enough about your blasted brochure! No one else wants
to read it."

Cecily giggled.

Jacob's face fell a little, but Alix smiled brightly and
said, "I enjoyed the brochure as well. It is a very good
one, I think."

"It is a very good brochure," Jacob agreed, suddenly
cheerful again. "So much useful information."

Rosalind was only half listening to them. "I do hope
that nothing is amiss," she said quietly. "He seemed very
angry about something."

That was understating what they'd all just witnessed.
Inspector Bauer had seemed positively enraged. Surely
that was not a good sign on the first night of their journey,
and it only made her feel even more ill at ease.

"I am certain there is no trouble," Erich offered with a
warm smile. "If there were, somebody would tell us."

Rosalind doubted that very much. In fact, she suspected that if there was trouble, she would be the last
to hear of it, if only to avoid a panic. She was Mister
Wallace's daughter. The crew would protect her from a
terrible truth at all costs—unless it came to an emergency
evacuation, in which case she'd no doubt be first aboard a
submersible. But there was no reason to argue the point.
Or to think about such an awful scenario.

"Of course," she said. "You're quite right, Herr Steiner."

She ate a little more chicken before saying, "And tell me, are you also a soldier?"

This time Jacob laughed. "No, no, Erich is in the family business."

Erich sighed. "Do not listen to him. He does not know what he is talking about."

"What sort of family business?" Rosalind asked.

"My father owns a steel factory," Erich said. "After I finish university, he wishes me to work for him there." He spread his hands. "But I have no interest in manufacturing. I wish to go into politics, not into business."

That did not surprise Rosalind. She could certainly imagine him in political office.

"Oh, ho!" Jacob laughed. "Yes, say that, my friend, but you will still take your father's tickets."

"What?" Cecily asked.

Erich sighed and explained, "My father's company helped build the railway, so we did not have to pay for our passage."

"Really?" Rosalind asked, careful to hide the extent of her curiosity.

"Yes, yes," Erich said. "My father provided the chromium steel for the tunnel we are traveling in. It is, my father says, impervious to salt water corrosion. And I certainly hope that is true." He paused. "I have no wish to go swimming in the North Atlantic in the middle of the night."

"How very unadventurous of you," Rosalind said.

"There's something you and Rose have in common, you know," Cecily said.

Erich raised an eyebrow and asked, "Sea bathing?"

"Both of your fathers are responsible for the railway," Cecily corrected. "Rosalind's father built the train."

"By himself?" Erich joked. "It must have taken him a long while."

Rosalind allowed herself a chuckle. "What she means is that he *owns* it." But she was privately irritated that Cecily had pointed out that she was the daughter of the man who owned the train. Now she had no choice but to embrace the label. "My father is Alexander Wallace, the industrialist," she explained, with a quick glare at Cecily. "He owns the Transatlantic Railway."

Erich and Jacob exchanged grins with each other.

"Very fortunate indeed that we were seated here!" Jacob exclaimed. "I cannot wait to write home about this. Such an exciting journey. So many new and interesting people to meet."

"Well," Cecily said, looking away, "one considers it impolite to brag . . ."

"One does," Rosalind agreed under her breath. "*You* do not."

Chapter Six

Bidding good night to Erich and Jacob proved more difficult than Rosalind would have wished. They lingered over the table, perhaps hoping one of Rosalind's companions would suggest they meet again tomorrow, or prolong an already exhausting day.

If Charles had been there, the boys wouldn't have joined them for dinner at all. She hadn't regretted their company, but Charles's absence was almost too outrageous to be believed. Perhaps it was an elaborate joke at her expense. How could he be so irresponsible as to abandon them at the very last minute, no matter what the reason? He could have tracked them down on the platform before they'd departed. What he had done was cowardly.

"Would the ladies like some ice cream?" Jacob asked as they stood.

"I must declare the evening finished," Rosalind stated firmly. "No offense to our new friends," she added with a smile at Cecily, "but it is growing rather late and it has already been a very busy day."

"Oh, pooh," Cecily said, pouting.

"Have you forgotten that I'm your chaperone?" Rosalind said, playing the one card she had.

"I am beginning to regret that now," Cecily grumbled.

"It is late, isn't it?" said Jacob. "I think bed sounds very sensible."

"You have no sense of fun, Jacob," Erich said.

Jacob laughed. "I have plenty of fun. But I am . . . an early morning person. It is the military life, you know? Up at dawn every day."

"Poor you," Cecily said absently. "Well, I hope that we shall see you both again tomorrow."

Erich flashed a dazzling smile at Rosalind. "It is a small train. I think we can safely say that our paths will cross again."

"Good evening, ladies," Jacob said. "Until tomorrow. Come along, Erich. Do not make a nuisance of yourself."

Rosalind sighed as she watched them go. She shook her head. The trouble with charming men was that one could never be certain if they were sincere or not. Of course, it was rather cynical of her to think such things. But there *was* the very friendly way Erich had looked at her. And even she had to admit, whether it was sincere or not, it was not altogether unpleasant. That was rather an understatement, truth be told . . .

"I think they're splendid," Cecily announced in the silence.

"I am inclined to agree," said Alix. "Especially that Lieutenant Hoffmeyer. He is very . . ." She paused, looking for the word.

"Mmm," Cecily hummed. "He is, isn't he?"

"Cecily!" Rosalind demanded. When there was no reply, she waved her hand in front of Cecily's face. "Cecily?"

"Hmm? Yes?"

"Please don't go losing your head."

"You're one to talk, Rose," Cecily said in her old impish voice. "I saw how you looked at Herr Steiner. It was positively disgraceful. Almost as disgraceful as the way he looked at *you*." She wagged a finger under Rosalind's nose. "You're our chaperone, remember? Whatever would my brother say if he found out?"

Rosalind's eyes smoldered. "I hardly think that Charles would have either right or reason to say anything," she answered, speaking a little too quickly. She caught her breath and straightened her shoulders. "But as you bring him up—"

"As you say, it is time for bed," Cecily interrupted in a singsong voice. "Alix, why don't you and I walk Rose to her room? It's the only decent thing to do given how good she's been about chaperoning us, don't you agree?"

"Yes, very good about it," Alix agreed. "And I am very grateful for it, you know. I am meeting an aunt at the station in America, but my family assumed there would be no need for a chaperone during the journey. It is so nice of you to look out for Cecily and myself. So very nice."

"No, no, Alix," Cecily groaned. "Rose isn't *actually* our chaperone. We're all scandalously unattended. That's the point. It's half the fun. I thought you understood."

Alix suddenly turned bright pink. "Oh, dear. We are not going to get into trouble with the train crew, are we?"

Rosalind held her tongue. She decided, once again, that no matter how much Cecily kept irritating her, her friend was just trying to make the best of a bad situation. So she laughed and took Alix by the arm. "No," she said, "we're not. Especially if Cecily remembers how to behave in public."

"And what precisely have I done that was so improper?" Cecily asked, feigning offense.

"You mean besides inviting strange men to sit at our table?" Rosalind countered.

"I didn't invite them. I obliged them at the head steward's request."

"Did you, really?" Rosalind said, grinning at Cecily. "Only the head steward didn't say so himself, did he?" Rosalind said. "For all we know, that was just a cunning ruse to impose their rather delightful company on us."

Cecily gave a look of mock astonishment. "No!" she gasped. "Oh, Rose! I certainly hadn't thought of that possibility!"

Alix's eyes went wide. She glanced between the two of them. "You . . . You don't think that they were lying to us, do you?" she asked.

Cecily laughed aloud. "Oh, Alix," she said. "Oh, beautiful, innocent Alix."

"What?" Alix said.

"Of course they were lying," Cecily continued. "'Sent by the head steward' my foot. No, clearly they saw the three most beautiful girls on the whole train—"

"Let's just say the entire dining car," Rosalind corrected, laughing now. "I wouldn't want us to get ahead of ourselves."

"—and decided that they simply had to dine with us," Cecily finished. "So they concocted the whole story. And a good thing, too; otherwise, we might never have met them. I think it's rather in their favor that they decided to meet us tonight, rather than leave a meeting to chance."

Agreed, Rosalind thought.

✿   ✿   ✿

Alone in her room, Rosalind found herself struck by a dreadful bout of insomnia. Part of it, she knew, was the excitement of the day: meeting new boys, meeting Alix, managing Cecily—and of course, a small amount of apprehension at being confined underwater for a whole week. But mostly, it was Charles.

Perhaps Charles had a secret lover in Hamburg whom he had gone to meet, and the entire trip had been a pretense to make the visit possible. It was perfectly sensible, Rosalind thought, much more sensible than being called away for some crisis to "defend the realm," or whatever lie Cecily had spun. Cecily was being evasive about the truth to spare her feelings, which was silly because she didn't have any feelings on the matter . . .

Rosalind caught a glimpse of herself in the mirror and shook her head.

"You don't really believe that, do you?" she asked aloud.

Best not to answer. Whenever she couldn't sleep, there was but one solution.

Read a book before bedtime.

Rosalind put her shoes on and left for the library car.

Most of the train was deserted. She passed only two people in the corridor, both of whom reeked of spirits and looked like they were headed to bed. The library was empty save for the librarian on duty. He wore a plain suit, not any sort of official train uniform, and looked barely awake, scarcely paying her any mind as he read some German magazine. But Rosalind was in no mood for conversation, either. She went to the English language shelves and selected a volume of Dickens. That would be the thing.

"May I take this to my compartment?" she asked the librarian.

He glanced up at her and didn't even try to smile. His eyes were puffy. He stifled a yawn. "You will have to sign for it," he said, pointing to a ledger on his desk. "Only I'm out of ink. I'll have to fetch more."

Rosalind exhaled slowly, annoyed by his attitude. She was half tempted to tell him that she was Alexander Wallace's daughter. She suspected that he wouldn't treat her so dismissively if he knew that, or if she were older, or a man. But it was hardly worth arguing with the staff over such a small slight.

"I'll read it here, thank you," she said.

"Very good, Miss." He closed his eyes and leaned back in his chair.

What sort of people was Father employing? Rosalind sincerely hoped that the daytime librarian had a better command of his manners. And his wardrobe. Perhaps they had put this fellow on at night assuming that no one would come looking for a book . . . As she stared at his suit, she realized that its drabness was familiar. Hadn't he been the man with Inspector Bauer in the dining car? But no, that was a silly thought. Why would a librarian be chasing after the chief of security? Maybe nondescript dress was preferred, or even mandated, for those who weren't porters or conductors or waitstaff.

Shaking her head to herself, Rosalind settled into one of the armchairs to read a few chapters of *Little Dorrit*. But she couldn't concentrate, and the words swam before her on the pages. She wasn't drowsy in the least.

Presently she felt that she was being watched. At first she scarcely noticed, chalking it up to fantasy or exhaustion. But the prickling feeling wouldn't go away. Soon she became quite certain that she and the librarian weren't alone.

She glanced up from her book. The librarian was at his desk, reading his magazine and ignoring her. Otherwise the room was deserted. She pushed herself out of the chair and marched for the exit, pulled the door sideways, and stepped out into the corridor. But the corridor was empty as well.

"Hmph," Rosalind said aloud. At long last, she was feeling tired again. She hurried back to her room, and only when she arrived did she realize she still held the book in her hands.

I ought to return it, she thought. *Before there's trouble.*

Then again, she could bring it back the following morning. She doubted the librarian would notice. And besides, if he did, she could claim that she was just making sure he was doing his job, on orders from her father. *That* would teach him not to be so rude and dismissive.

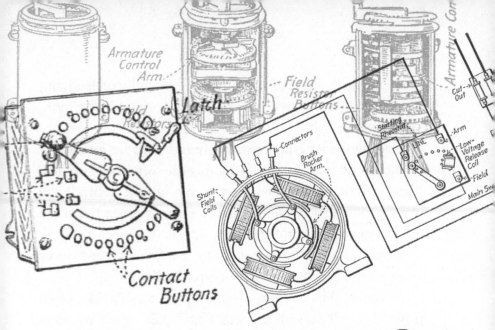

The next morning, Rosalind awoke late. She couldn't even remember what time she had finally gone to sleep. Her bleary eyes fell on the Dickens on her nightstand. Indeed, without the arrival of Doris, Cecily's maid, she may well have slept right through until lunchtime.

"Sorry to bother you, Miss," Doris kept apologizing, vainly trying to mask her Cockney accent. "But I'm here at Lady de Vere's request."

With Doris's help, Rosalind rose, washed, and dressed. Not that she required any assistance, but Cecily had apparently demanded that Doris do so, and it seemed to make the girl happy, or at least less uncomfortable. However hard Mother had tried to instill proper values in her, Rosalind simply could not understand having someone *else* put on her clothes for her. That was her greatest vice, in Mother's eyes: self-reliance. Of course, it was extremely difficult putting on a corset by oneself, but that only made figuring out a better option all the more appealing.

Poor Doris was appropriately horrified to see Rosalind's choice of undergarments—notably the soft cotton bodice, firm in structure but without even a hint of boning. She gaped for a few moments before remembering her place and snapping her mouth shut.

Rosalind almost laughed. "Don't tell me you've never seen an emancipation waist before, Doris."

"Course, Miss," Doris replied with a nervous glance toward the door, as if she was afraid they might be overheard.

"I suspect it's rather like what you wear," Rosalind added as she put on her blouse.

That would be the real cause of Doris's distress: the violation of class differences. It was all so silly, really.

Doris nodded quickly. "Yes, Miss. Right you are, Miss." She hesitated and took a step toward Rosalind, reaching out with one hand. "Miss, are you certain you'd not prefer me to—"

"I . . . would . . . not," Rosalind interrupted, punctuating each word with the fastening of a button. She studied herself in the mirror for a moment. "You see, the marvelous thing about the emancipation waist is that one can put it on all by oneself, without needing help. But of course, you already know that."

"Yes, Miss," Doris said sheepishly, as if she'd entered some grand conspiracy and was about to get into trouble for it.

Rosalind then selected a narrow purple necktie from her illicit supply. She suspected that Cecily would have words with her on the matter, but this was precisely the look she wanted for the day. After all, the jacket she had selected—purple and white with narrow stripes—was cut with the collar open, so it would be simply absurd not to wear something around the neck.

"Doris," she said, catching a glimpse of the girl's troubled expression in the mirror. "You needn't worry so. No one is going to know that I dressed myself. I won't tell anyone if you don't."

"Yes, Miss," Doris said, bowing her head.

"I expect you're wondering if I have a maid of my own."

"Yes, I . . ." Doris glanced up and stopped herself. Looking down again, she said, "Not my place to wonder, Miss."

Rosalind sighed, but kept cheerful. One day, women would dress themselves. One day, these class distinctions would be set on fire. Had her father not made his own fortune, he might very well be a manservant. There was dignity in service; he'd said so himself. It was one of the few points she and her father agreed upon, despite the hypocritical airs he now affected. Doris was simply doing a job, like a tradesman or a doctor. But it was just another reminder of what had irked her most during her stay in England: that she could not speak candidly to maids without fear of being "too familiar."

"Well, I do have a maid," she said. "Her name is Lucy and she is simply splendid. The two of you are going to get on wonderfully."

Lucy had been with the family for the better part of five years, beginning as a housemaid. Later, she'd become Rosalind's attendant more or less at Rosalind's insistence, as Lucy shared a rebellious streak that she kept carefully hidden. They had a simple arrangement: when it came time to dress Rosalind—barring any circumstance in which she actually required assistance—Lucy would read magazines and chat about the servants' hall gossip. Rosalind dreaded to think what would become of Lucy if she ever sought employment elsewhere.

"I 'spect so, Miss," Doris said, smiling a little.

"Now then." Rosalind pulled on her jacket and fussed over her skirt to be sure everything was properly in place. "Hats . . . hats . . . hats . . . So many to choose from."

Doris, clearly relieved to be of help, rushed to fetch the hatboxes. She glanced back, confused.

"There's only three, Miss," she said.

Rosalind grinned. "Like I said, so many hats to choose from. I sometimes think I ought to reduce the number to one and simply change the feathers from time to time. Or! Or I could wear a bicycle suit . . . No, that's a terrible idea."

Doris blinked a few times and giggled. She clamped a hand over her mouth. "Pardon, Miss. As you say, Miss."

Rosalind grinned at Doris, determined to reassure the girl. But before she could say anything, she heard a bell chime softly. She looked in the direction of the noise and saw a new cylinder sitting in the tray of the pneumatic post machine.

"Just a moment," she told Doris as she hurried to retrieve the message.

"Course, Miss."

Rosalind opened the cylinder and read the note inside. It was from Cecily, of course—who else would be sending her letters? It was an invitation to tea and possibly sandwiches in the Red Parlor at her earliest convenience.

"Doris," she said, "as you can see, I have everything well in hand. Why don't you go along and tell Cecily that I'll meet her in the Red Parlor in, shall we say, an hour? I have a book that needs returning to the library."

"Yes, Miss," Doris said with a nod. She backed toward the door. "And will that be all, Miss?"

"Yes, absolutely," Rosalind answered. "Thank you, Doris; you've been such a help. And remember . . ." She placed her fingertip to her lips. "I won't tell if you don't tell."

Doris flashed a hesitant smile. "Yes, Miss," she said. She hurried out of the room as if she couldn't depart fast enough. Back to the dreary, formal servitude she at least knew and understood.

Rosalind turned back to the mirror and tested the look of her hat. No doubt this choice would bother Cecily, just as her behavior with Doris would have. But Cecily would never know about *that*, would she?

o   o   o

An hour later, Rosalind found Cecily and Alix waiting for her in the Red Parlor, seated beside one of the long windows. They stared curiously at the water rushing past them. She was glad they had picked this spot.

Everything in the compartment was done in crimson or burgundy, all of it accented with gold. It was a nice contrast to the blues found elsewhere in the train.

Cecily rose from her chair.

"Good morning, Rose." After a perfunctory hug, she stepped back. "I trust you slept well. You look lovely. Doris has done a marvelous job with you . . ." Her eyes suddenly widened. "Good Lord, you're wearing a tie."

"Good morning to you, too," Rosalind replied good-naturedly, leaning in again to kiss her friend on the cheek.

Cecily sank back into the velvety cushions. "Rose, why must you insist on dressing like a man? I thought I had broken you of that habit in London."

"I am not dressing like a man," Rosalind said, though she'd predicted Cecily would say precisely that. "I am wearing a skirt."

"Lots of men wear skirts," Cecily said matter-of-factly.

"Those are called kilts, Cecily," Rose replied, sighing.

"Don't you dare turn Scottish on me, Rosalind," Cecily protested. "I won't have it."

Alix cleared her throat softly and leaned forward. "I think it looks very charming on you, Rose," she said. "And it goes with your hat."

"Thank you, Alix," Rosalind replied, holding her chin up. She grinned at Cecily and motioned to Alix. "See?"

Cecily pouted and crossed her arms. "You're all conspiring against me," she declared. "First Alix puts peacock feathers in her hat. Then Rose wears a necktie. What next?"

Rosalind shot a quick glance at Alix. The girl did indeed

have peacock feathers in her hat, and her entire ensemble was similarly a luxuriant mixture of blue and green. Even her hatpins were shaped like little peacock feathers.

"I think you look lovely, Alix," she said, and she meant it. "Besides, I thought you liked peacock feathers, Cecily."

"I do," Cecily said. "I was going to wear *my* peacock feather hat today. I was forced to change everything when she called on me for breakfast."

"Yes," Rosalind said dully. "It would be foolish to think that two people on the same train could wear feathers at the same time."

Cecily turned to Alix and raised her hands. "You see? Rose understands. Alix said I was being silly."

Rosalind exchanged a look with Alix, who was trying very hard to avoid laughing. Cecily seemed not to notice, distracted as she was with the great pleasure of being indignant.

"Did you have a pleasant night, Alix?" Rosalind asked, for fear she might laugh, too, if she didn't engage in conversation.

"Oh, yes, very pleasant," Alix said. "I listened to the gramophone for a little while and I dropped off to sleep almost immediately. And you?"

"I read a book and I enjoyed it so much that I stole it from the library," Rosalind answered.

Cecily clapped her hands. "How utterly wicked of you. It almost makes up for the necktie. Almost."

"Oh, hush," Rosalind told her, but her tone was soft. "Now then, what is on the itinerary for today?"

Alix began thumbing through her brochure. "Goodness,

I was not aware they had included an itinerary," she said, sounding a little embarrassed.

"She doesn't mean it literally, silly," Cecily said with a playful swat at her friend. She looked at Rosalind. "Well, I have just ordered some tea and sandwiches—"

"Brandenburg," Alix interrupted, her face buried in the brochure.

"Pardon?" Cecily asked, annoyed.

"Today we stop at Brandenburg for lunch," Alix explained, reading. "And we are there for the afternoon . . . and for dinner . . . Oh! And then we have a ball." She smiled and shoved the brochure back into her handbag. "This will be a fun day, I think."

"A ball?" Cecily's eyes glittered. "I do so enjoy a good ball." She blinked a few times. "I wonder where they'll put the dance floor. I don't think there will be room for everyone."

"I believe the ball will be *off* the train, when we stop at Brandenburg," Rosalind explained, as patiently as she could.

"Now that makes no sense at all," Cecily said. Her gaze wandered back to the window. "Brandenburg's in Germany—even I know that. And we've already left Germany."

"No, Brandenburg Station," Rosalind corrected. "We stop at three stations in the Atlantic along the way. Brandenburg's the first, then Neptune, and finally Columbia." She paused and frowned. "I already told you all of this, Cecily. Honestly, you don't pay attention to anything, do you?"

"Very rarely," Cecily said, sounding rather proud about it.

"Especially when it comes to matters of railway transportation," Alix said.

Rosalind smirked. "They obviously can't keep us cooped up in a train for seven days without giving us some time to get out and stretch our legs, now can they?"

"I suppose not," Cecily replied. "Well, in that case, when we arrive we simply must go for a walk. Oh, and we must decide what we're all going to wear to the ball. And Rosalind, you must allow me to help you with this decision. I am quite afraid of what you'll wear if I don't."

○ ○ ○

Over tea and sandwiches, Rosalind found herself drifting further and further away from the conversation. Talk of fashion turned to snide, hushed observations on the ladies sitting about the parlor, their poor choices of dresses and jewels. Before long, Alix and Cecily were whispering to each other about a duchess she'd never heard of and the ghastly thing she had decided to wear to some ball or other in London, or Paris, or Vienna.

She'd expected as much from Cecily, but she'd rather hoped Alix would be different, given the love of books and curiosity about machinery she'd hinted at yesterday. But as the train neared Brandenburg Station, it became increasingly clear that Alix was exactly like so many of the aristocrats and debutantes Rosalind had met that spring in London. She had felt out of place there, too, of course, but at least Cecily and Charles had taken great efforts to include her in whatever they were doing. And being an exotic American heiress had at least kept her in the social orbit of Cecily's class. But now, in more private company, she suddenly felt forgotten.

That was the trouble with being "exotic"; in the end, you would never truly belong. In Old Money's eyes, it was bad enough having a self-made father—having a respectable mother did only so much to ameliorate that—and Rosalind simply couldn't bring herself to put on the necessary charade to convince her aristocratic companions that she was "one of them." She *didn't* belong. Mother certainly didn't drive motorcars or ask to attend rallies with Aunt Mildred. Apparently proper girls weren't at all interested in getting the vote. Cecily and Alix were living proof.

As she stared absently at the fish swimming about outside the window, Rosalind suddenly noticed a peculiar shape lurking in the distance. It was dimly lit and barely visible, but it was definitely *there*. She squinted, struggling to make sense of it. Was it a whale? It was long, almost cylindrical, sharp at the front, and possessed of several peculiar protrusions. Most astonishingly, it kept pace with them. Surely no animal could do that.

She leaned forward a little.

"Rose?" Cecily said.

Rosalind almost jumped, having been ignored for so long. "Hmm, yes?" She turned away from the window with a smile. Best not to let them think that she had been sulking or anything.

"What are you looking at?" Cecily asked.

"Oh, there was something . . ." Rosalind glanced back out the window. But the shape, whatever it had been, was gone. "A whale, I think. Maybe."

"A whale?" Alix said. "That is very exciting. I am surprised you can see anything at all out there. But you should be talking with us, not gawking at things outside, yes? We are much more fun."

"Yes, much," Cecily agreed, though with a pointed stare.

"Well, that's true," Rosalind said, trying very hard to mean it.

In a stroke of luck, the train began to slow at that very moment. It was barely noticeable at first, but Cecily and Alix could sense it, too. The two girls' faces darted to the window. Evidently the engineer was doing his best to avoid unsettling the passengers with an abrupt stop.

"Ah!" Cecily exclaimed. "What fun! Sightseeing time! Now then, I must get back to my room and fetch a parasol before we go."

Rosalind sighed. "There's no need for a parasol, Cecily," she said. "We're underwater, remember? There's no sun."

Cecily flashed an indignant look. "It's not for the sun, Rose. It's to complement my hat."

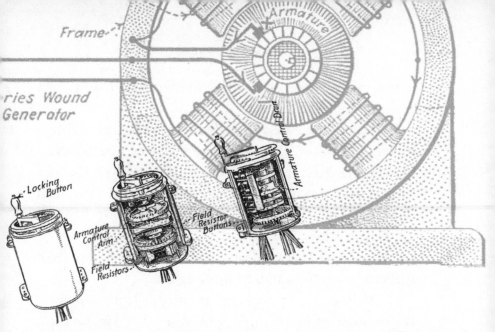

As the passengers readied themselves to enter the undersea train station, Rosalind's expectations were informed by her father's sketches once again, although she had paid very little attention to them. Undersea architecture was boring. Bicycles were interesting. The Hamburg terminus should have prepared her for what was in store, but as she stepped out of the train onto the platform . . . Rosalind was struck dumb.

The circular grand concourse was three stories high with an arched ceiling of glass—more like a palace of gold and crystal than a railway station. A large balcony extended out from the second floor, three quarters of the way around, facing the train platform. Preparations for the ball had already been made, with dozens of tables draped with white cloths, lit by electric lamps in the shape of candles, and festooned with vases of flowers.

And then there was the eagle theme. They were everywhere. There were bronze statues of eagles, and eagles on banners hanging down from the balcony. Even the vast marble floor was marked by a grand mosaic of a German imperial eagle, though the effect was rather lost beneath all the furniture.

"A bouquet of nationalism," Rosalind mused, once she'd gathered herself enough to speak again.

Cecily craned her neck and pointed, silently counting the number of German flags on display. "'Tis, isn't it?" Then she chuckled. "Less of a bouquet, really; more of an onslaught. You'd think the Germans were afraid we might forget they owned the place."

The passengers filing off the train had started to find seats at the various tables. Rosalind hurried forward, gesturing for the girls to follow. "It really is a bit much," she said as they maneuvered through the crowd. She had to raise her voice in order to be heard over the dull echo of the chatter swirling around the vast room. "The station is quite pretty, but all of this . . . nonsense does distract from the ambience, don't you find?"

"I couldn't have put it better myself," Cecily said.

Once seated, they found menus printed on embossed paper: a list of what would be provided rather than a selection of options. Of course, that was only to be expected, Rosalind knew. Everything they ate had to be shipped down in quantity beforehand, and it could hardly be kept for weeks on end. One shipment for each voyage, probably. It was enough of an extravagance that they were being treated to meals in the station at all . . .

"Hmmm," Cecily said. "I could do with a little more variety, but I suppose that's that." She placed the menu back on the table and frowned at a nearby eagle statue. "I wonder if they'll wheel out a statue of the Kaiser at some point."

Rosalind laughed. "I almost expect them to start playing the 'Deutschlandlied' while we dine."

Cecily giggled and turned to Alix, but Alix did not look pleased.

"It's not very funny, you know," she said quietly.

"What isn't?" Rosalind asked. She was aghast that she'd somehow offended her new friend. She was also quite confused. Admitting she was a would-be suffragette hadn't done it, but poking fun at their surroundings had?

"Well, I don't think either of you is being very fair," Alix said. "I mean, yes, it is very . . . extravagant. I am not entirely pleased by the display."

"The eagles, you mean?" Rosalind ventured.

Alix nodded, her frown fading. "By those least of all," she concurred. "But we Germans aren't the only people who love absurd pageantry like this. The English are just as bad."

Cecily responded with a carefree toss of her head. "Well, perhaps just a bit."

"And I do not know about you Americans," Alix said to Rosalind. "But from what I hear, you're not entirely blameless in this regard."

"Oh, yes," Rosalind said, relieved the tense moment

had passed. "We enjoy our flags and eagles as well. So you can have a good laugh at my expense when we arrive in Columbia Station at the end of the week. I daresay it will be even more ridiculous than all of this. Agreed?"

Alix finally smiled. "Agreed. To be fair, it is rather silly, isn't it? Pride?"

"Utterly," Cecily said.

"Well, seeing as how the German government bank-rolled the construction, you can't blame them for being proud, now can you?" Rosalind suggested, mostly as a peace offering to Alix.

But Cecily simply tossed her head again. "I can blame anyone for anything," she said. "I'm English. It's the rules."

◇   ◇   ◇

After lunch, in order to avoid the crowds, Rosalind led Cecily and Alix up to the second-floor balcony. Rose and Alix stared down at the mass of people below, but for some reason Cecily had turned her back on the view.

"What are all these doors here?" Cecily asked, pointing to a series of bulkhead hatches that lined the dim hallway behind them.

Rosalind glanced over her shoulder. "Submersibles," she replied.

"No, they are certainly doors," Alix insisted.

Rosalind laughed and replied, "No, what I mean is that they lead to submersibles. Those are the escape hatches."

"Escape hatches?" Cecily asked.

"Of course." Rosalind couldn't tell if Cecily's blithe confusion was an act. But perhaps it was. "We're underneath the ocean. If something . . . untoward were to happen . . . flooding or something . . . we would need a means of escape, and quickly. Especially now, when everybody is off of the train."

Alix strode to one of the doors and peered at it. "How many are there?" she asked.

"Enough for all of us, I should hope," Rosalind said.

"I suppose it would be rather awkward if there happened to be a shortage of seats," Cecily said in a dry voice. "Although I expect we three would be fine. Women and children first, you know."

"You're full of charitable feeling, Cecily," Rosalind joked.

A shadow passed just outside her range of vision. When she turned, her smile vanished. There was a man at the end of the hallway, watching them: a man with a mustache, in a plain brown suit and a matching bowler hat. Rosalind recognized him almost immediately. He was the one who had been staring at her from the crowd in Hamburg.

"Oh, goodness," Cecily whispered, following Rosalind's gaze.

"Is he watching us?" Alix murmured.

Rosalind glanced toward the balcony, then back down the hall. He was definitely watching them. And they were all alone up here. "Cecily, get behind me," she said.

"What does he want?" Cecily asked, her voice rising to a whimper. "Why is he looking at us so?"

"I don't know," Rosalind said softly. "Just stay back."

She stepped forward and fixed him with a hard glare, then addressed him in a loud voice: "Is there something you want from us, Sir?"

The man jerked slightly, as if startled out of a trance. He looked from side to side, just in case there were some grounds for doubt as to whom Rosalind had spoken.

"Yes, I am speaking to you," Rosalind said, taking another half step forward. "What do you want?"

"I . . . am lost," the man said. He grinned rather unpleasantly from under his mustache. "You can . . . help me, yes?" He took a few steps in their direction.

Out of the corner of her eye, Rosalind glimpsed Alix pulling one of the long pins from her hat. She held it out like a dagger. That was some decent thinking. Hopefully it wouldn't come to that, but the hatpin was certainly a reliable weapon in a pinch.

"Rose, he's coming over here," Cecily gasped. "Why is he coming over here?"

"Shh." Rosalind stepped forward again, closing the distance between them. She didn't relish the idea of being near the fellow, whatever his game was, but she certainly didn't want him anywhere near Cecily or Alix. "Sir, if you are lost, kindly turn around and walk in the other direction. You will find the stairs leading to the platform almost immediately."

"Oh, yes, but—"

"We do not know you," Rosalind interrupted, "nor have we any wish to make your acquaintance. Turn around and leave us in peace, or I will have no choice but to shout for help."

The man quickly held out his hands and said, "Oh, but you misunderstand me . . ."

"If that is true, then you will kindly demonstrate your good intentions by leaving at once," Rosalind shouted.

"I go! I go!" With an angry scowl, he began backing away. As he reached the adjoining hallway, he very nearly collided with Jacob, who was rounding the corner with Erich. The man jumped back. But then he planted himself in front of the boys and began shouting angrily in German.

Jacob stiffened, clearly at a loss as to how to respond. He suddenly looked very young in his crisp uniform. Erich straightened and smoothed the lapels of his suit jacket, but at that moment he spotted the three girls down the hall. His expression clouded. He whirled and gave the strange man a shove toward the stairs. *"Dummkopf!"* he snapped. "Have you been bothering these ladies?"

"Wah, I . . . *nein,"* the man stammered.

"Go away before my friend and I give you something to think about!"

"I go," the man growled again.

He stumbled around the corner and vanished from sight. Rosalind held her breath, watching Erich and Jacob watch *him*, making sure he'd descended the stairs. When they turned back toward the girls, Rosalind finally exhaled. She took Cecily's hand. It was trembling slightly. Or maybe it was her own hand that was quivering.

"See, Cecily?" Rosalind soothed. "The trouble's all passed."

"I didn't even get to use my pin," Alix muttered, placing

it delicately back inside her hat. She almost sounded disappointed.

Rosalind managed a nervous smile. She didn't like to think how close they may have come to needing it. "A neat trick, that," she said. "You'll have to teach me sometime."

"I will," Alix said, cocking an eyebrow. "Mother says every young lady should learn how to give a swift kick and a good stab."

Cecily let go of Rosalind's hand. "She's more practical than my mother." Cecily had put on her usual unruffled expression, but Rosalind could see that she was still shaky.

"And mine," Rosalind said, with one eye on Erich and Jacob, who were now rushing down the hall toward them. "Thank you for the rescue, gentlemen," she called. "It was very good of you."

Jacob blushed a little at the compliment. "Well, it is a gentleman's duty, you know," he said.

"Oh, I don't know," Erich said with a nod toward the girls. "We're pleased to help, of course, but I wonder how much we were truly required. He seemed about to flee for his life."

Rosalind shook her head. "Nonsense. I don't know what might have happened if the two of you hadn't arrived."

"Oh, don't be so modest, Rose," Cecily countered. "You were simply marvelous, glaring at him like Boudicca staring down the Roman hordes." She blinked at Erich and pointed to Rosalind, mouthing the word *"Marvelous!"*

"I did not know the Romans had hordes," Alix mused aloud.

"Well, there's obviously been a bit of a muddle," Cecily said, interrupting the conversation before it became too peculiar. "What matters is we have found you, and you us, and that awful man is gone."

"Right," Erich agreed. "Besides, who cares about the Romans when we have the English?"

"How *did* you two happen to find us?" Rosalind asked. Now that Cecily had mentioned it, this struck her as a strange coincidence.

"We were looking for you," Jacob said. "The three of you," he quickly corrected. "It was Erich's idea."

"No, no," Erich said with a laugh. "It was my idea to come up here. We could not find you in the crowd so I suggested we take a look from the balcony."

"And a good thing, too," Cecily said coyly.

"Why were you looking for us?" Alix asked. Apparently she was not interested in joining in on Cecily's flirtations in the least. *Mother would like this girl*, Rosalind thought. "We will be at the ball tonight. Surely you would see us then."

Erich coughed a little and exchanged looks with Jacob.

"Is it not obvious?" Jacob asked Alix. "Erich and I would like to ask you girls to join us for dinner."

"Oh!" Alix exclaimed, turning bright red. "Oh, my goodness. I don't think we could."

"But we must," Cecily insisted.

Rosalind hid a smile. "Speaking as the chaperone," she said in a mock authoritative tone, like a haughty governess, "I think it would only be polite to accept the invitation." After all, what harm could there be? They had already been seen dining in the company of these two fellows. Any gossip that might come of it was already swirling about the train in the way gossip did, like tendrils of cigarette smoke. No doubt they would catch a whiff of it before they arrived in the United States, where Mother and Father would be apprised. No, the girls might as well enjoy themselves now. The damage was done.

"You will?" Erich said, sounding surprised. He quickly recovered his easy smile. "You will. Well, that's wonderful. Good. That is to say, it's good."

"We'll speak to the head steward to make the arrangements," Jacob added.

"Lovely. What time do we eat?" Rosalind asked.

"Four o'clock," Alix answered. "So that we all have plenty of time to change for the ball afterward."

Rosalind blinked. "Change for the ball? We're already dressing for dinner. How many times are we changing today?"

"Twice by the schedule," Cecily said. "But I'm hoping for more. I've brought so many dresses, I don't know if I shall have occasion to wear them all."

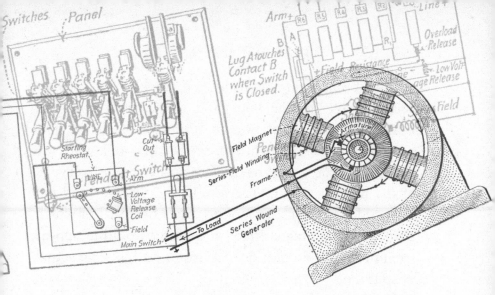

Rosalind thought about not changing for dinner and saving the effort for the ball. Mother would be horrified at the notion, which made it all the more appealing. But then she remembered her father's letter: "The public will judge you." Meaning "the public will judge the family." If Rosalind flouted convention too much, too openly here on the train, her parents would be furious. They might never let her out of Pittsburgh again, at least not until she was married.

So Rosalind changed into something simple and understated: a pale-green evening dress that demanded as little effort as possible. Better to be comfortable than fashionable, she reasoned. But once she and Cecily and Alix were seated with Jacob and Erich over carrot soup, fillet of salmon, and game fowl, she began to regret her decision.

Chapter Nine

Both Cecily and Alix had taken pains to make themselves pretty for the boys, and worse, both boys had done the same. Jacob was in uniform, of course, just as he had been the night before. Erich wore a white tie and dress coat, as did most of the other men. Everyone at the table—indeed, everyone in First Class—had put tremendous effort into looking their best. All of which had the unfortunate effect of making Rosalind appear even more like an outsider. Or worse still, like an actual chaperone.

By the time dessert sorbets and after-dinner chocolates were served, Rosalind had drifted completely out of the flirty, mindless conversation. The four laughed over a faux pas that some viscount had committed during a recent wedding ceremony between two aristocrats Rosalind had never heard of. She didn't recognize a single name. She couldn't follow, nor did she care to. *The lone American is indeed alone*, she thought.

Rosalind tried to soothe herself with the music of the orchestra. Wagner, of course, to complement the eagles, lest anyone forget the station had been built by the Germans. Her thoughts turned to Charles. He would have included her in the conversation, if only out of politeness. He always did. He should have been here. What had really happened to him? It made no sense.

She glanced at the train, parked alongside them. Only First Class passengers could dine in the station concourse; only they could be serenaded by the orchestra. Second Class had been allowed out earlier, to stretch their legs. Rather like cattle. For the meal they were confined to their own dining cars. The ball wasn't on their itinerary, either.

Rosalind sighed. She would have expected better of Father. He'd organized all of this, knowing his own family would have traveled Second Class if he hadn't proved himself a capable industrialist. Their Scottish cousins wouldn't be able to afford any ticket whatsoever; they would be porters or waitstaff if aboard at all. But perhaps the decision to adhere so firmly to class distinctions hadn't been Father's to make. He had Old Money partners with Old World priorities. He was obliged to follow their rules, and to pretend to respect their prejudices, for the sake of business. It was no small part of his success.

Oh, dash it all, she thought. If her foul mood got the better of her, this was going to be a very long journey, indeed.

○   ○   ○

The hour for the ball was approaching and Doris still hadn't arrived. Rosalind had spent the better part of two hours alone in her room, expecting Doris to come by at some point to "assist" her after she'd finished with Cecily. Not that Rosalind minded being left to dress on her own, of course. But Cecily could have made clearer that she would take longer than usual. Then again, Rosalind should have known that intuitively, given her friend's flirtations with Jacob. Alix certainly would have. But Alix had her own servant.

Left to her own devices, Rosalind chose her pink gown,

the one with the embroidered roses and the mother-of-pearl beading. Cecily would appreciate it. She always called it Rosalind's "rose dress"; "a rose for Rose," as she put it. Rosalind had worn it many times in London, and each time Cecily had pointed out how perfect the color was for her.

When the clock finally struck seven, Rosalind left her room. If she waited any longer, she reasoned, she might end up sitting there all night in her ball gown.

o   o   o

In the grand concourse, the tables and chairs had already been cleared, and wooden paneling had been laid atop the eagle mosaic to provide a suitable dance floor. Rosalind wished some of the other eagles could have been covered as well. A ball was no place for national pride. A ball was tailor-made for fun lovers like Cecily, as it should be. Rosalind looked this way and that for her friend among the swelling crowd of First Class passengers.

The orchestra began to tune their instruments. The dancing would start very soon . . .

Rosalind froze in place. She felt a curious sensation on the back of her neck. As if she was being watched, just as she'd felt in the library. Sure enough, she spotted the mustached man in the brown suit. He was staring right at her. When their eyes met, he shoved his way back through the crowd and into a Second Class car of the train, vanishing.

She took a few breaths to steady herself.

"Rose?" a voice cried.

Rosalind blinked rapidly several times and summoned the bravest smile she could. Alix, Erich, and Jacob swept toward her through the crowd. Erich in particular looked rather smart in his white tie and black suit. But she didn't even notice what the others were wearing until they reached her; she was too shaken.

"Hello, Alix," Rosalind said, holding her at arm's length. "You look lovely. Blue suits you, it really does."

Alix blushed and said, "Oh, well, thank you . . ."

Erich and Jacob both bowed to her in unison. Then Erich took a step forward and took her hand gently, bowing over it while he smiled at her.

"Fräulein Wallace," he said, letting her hand linger in his for a rather pleasant moment. "You look *wunderbar*, if you will permit my saying so. Truly . . . a rose, like your namesake."

Rosalind did her best to look poised and elegant, even as she felt her cheeks warming at the compliment. "Very kind of you to say, Herr Steiner."

"I am surprised at how cool it is here," Alix announced, gazing off toward the crowd. "I mean, with all the people. It's lovely, not at all stuffy like I thought it would be."

"It's all done with salt water," Rosalind said. She thought to explain further, but she found that Erich was still gazing at her, in a manner that she found both engaging and most uncomfortable. It made her tongue-tied. After a few moments, she forced herself back to her senses. "Have any of you seen Cecily? I'd have thought she would be here by now."

Jacob exchanged looks with Alix. Erich gave a slight shrug and looked back toward the train.

"I thought she was with you," Alix said. "I knocked on her door but she was not there."

Rosalind frowned and studied the crowd again.

"Perhaps she's fallen asleep," Erich ventured.

"Cecily? Asleep?" Rosalind shook her head. "You'd be hard-pressed to find her tired after a ball, and certainly not before one."

"Could she still be dressing?" Alix asked, though she sounded very skeptical. "She may not have heard me when I knocked, I suppose."

"Seems unlikely," Rosalind said. "I know the walls are soundproof, but she should still be able to hear a knock on the door."

Erich smiled and said, "Well, I wouldn't worry too much about it. I am certain she will arrive eventually. Uh . . . in the meantime . . ." He extended his hand toward Rosalind. "Could I perhaps have the next dance?"

Rosalind paused. He was smiling at her. The orchestra had just begun playing a waltz, "The Blue Danube." The music, the splendor of the ambiance, the rose-colored dress, the ball beneath the sea, this handsome boy asking for a dance . . . It all seemed like something from a fairy tale.

And suddenly she thought of Charles.

Rosalind hesitated and drew her hand back. Why had she thought about Charles? Aside from the fact that he'd abandoned her on this train? Yes, he was handsome. Yes, she was fond of him. And then thinking about Charles made her think about Cecily.

"No," she said.

Erich blinked in surprise.

"Not just yet," Rosalind quickly clarified. "I am so sorry, Erich, but I simply cannot enjoy the dance without knowing what has become of Cecily."

"Ah, of course," Erich said. He put on a smile. "Go, see to your friend. But do hurry back, yes?"

"I will, thank you," Rosalind said. As she turned to go, Alix took her arm and began walking with her.

"I am going with you," she whispered.

"But wouldn't you rather stay?" Jacob called after her.

Rosalind glanced back over her shoulder. "Steady on, gentlemen," she said. "The night is young, and we surely cannot monopolize you the whole time, now can we? Now do get us some punch for when we return."

o o o

After the first few knocks, there was still no answer from Cecily. Rosalind tried again several times, each louder than the last.

"Cecily?" she shouted. "Are you in there?"

Beside her, Alix pressed her ear up against the door. "I don't hear anything," she said. "Could she be elsewhere?"

"I suppose she may have gone to one of the other compartments, but why? And for that matter, where? The dining cars? We've already eaten. One of the parlors? Everyone is out in the station. The library?"

Alix smiled. "Yes, quite likely," she joked.

On a whim, Rosalind tried the door handle, though she

knew that it would be locked. Only it wasn't. Frowning, Rosalind slid the door open and stepped inside, with Alix following closely behind her.

Then she stopped.

Cecily was there. On the floor. Not moving. Not breathing. Eyes open and vacant. Her body was sprawled next to Doris's body, which lay a few paces away. Both were covered in blood—blood that had soaked the carpet and splattered against the walls and furnishings. Cecily was still in a state of undress. Her ball gown lay on the bed, waiting to be put on. Her jewelry was arrayed on a side table, waiting to adorn her. It seemed Doris had been doing Cecily's hair when . . `. whatever it was had happened.

Rosalind felt cold. She took a few uncertain steps toward the bodies. Alix held her back, clinging to her arm. Cecily's throat had been cut, and the cut had not been clean. Doris had been dispatched in much the same way.

Alix started to tremble, her hands clenching spasmodically into fists. She slowly looked up at Rosalind.

"Mein Gott!" she cried. "Cecily!"

And with that, she fainted dead away and fell into Rosalind's arms.

Armature Control Arm

Field Resistors

Latch

Field Resistor Buttons

Armature Con...

Cut-Out

Starting Rheostat

Connectors

Arm

Brush Rocker Arm

Low-Voltage Release Coil

Shunt Field Coils

Field

Main Switch

Contact Buttons

After that, everything became a blur.

A porter arrived, summoned by Alix's cry. The poor man retched from the sight and staggered back into the corridor. His scream of horror brought more men, of whom enough managed to keep their heads to usher Rosalind and Alix out of the room.

And then, quite suddenly it seemed, Rosalind was sitting on a sofa in one of the blue-and-gold parlors, comforting Alix.

The girl was sobbing into her shoulder. By God, Rosalind wanted to cry as well. But she found that she could not. She found herself unable to do anything but sit perfectly still, staring straight ahead while she stroked Alix's hair and murmured, "It's okay. It's okay. It's okay . . ."

Chapter Ten

She didn't even know what she was saying. All she could see were Cecily's dead eyes, staring at nothing, in a pool of blood . . .

The door opened.

Three men in suits entered the room and slammed the door behind them. Two took up position on either side of the exit, while the third—a middle-aged man with graying hair and a sour expression—removed his hat and approached. Rosalind recognized him instantly as the grim-faced Inspector Bauer who had disrupted dinner the previous evening. He'd looked furious then, and he looked furious now.

"What is going on?" Rosalind demanded, starting to rise.

"Sit!" Bauer snapped.

Rosalind was tempted to stand on principle, but she doubted that it would do much good. Obeying, she replied, "What do you want?"

"I am Inspector Bauer of the Hamburg Police," he answered, adjusting his tie.

"I know who you are," Rosalind said, and she repeated her question more firmly: "What do you want?"

"I am responsible for security on the train," Bauer told her. "And I have some questions to put to the both of you."

"Is this about Cecily's death?" Rosalind asked.

"I will ask the questions!" Bauer barked.

Rosalind tensed, torn between outrage and grief. How dare he speak to her like that! Her friend was *dead*. Beside her, Alix cringed, and Rosalind wrapped her arms around the girl to comfort her.

"Now then," Bauer said, "the two of you found the bodies?"

"Yes, that's right," Rosalind replied. She tried to keep a civil tone, though all she wanted was to shout back at him, to demand to know how he could have let such a thing happen. But she held her tongue.

"And you are . . . ?" Bauer asked.

"Rosalind Wallace."

If Bauer recognized her name, he did not show it.

"Alix von Hessen," Alix said softly.

"I did not hear you," Bauer growled, as if he assumed Alix's meekness was born of truculence rather than of shock and sorrow.

"*Alix von Hessen!*" Alix shrieked, burying her face in Rosalind's shoulder.

Bauer drew back. He muttered something under his breath. "You are related to the Grand Duke of Hesse?"

"My cousin," Alix murmured.

"I see," Bauer said quietly. He looked down at the floor, and then back up. "Perhaps you would care to retire to your compartment while I interview this young woman. There is no need for—"

"'This young woman'?" Alix snapped, suddenly sitting up and squaring her shoulders. "No, I am staying with Rosalind while you ask your questions. She and I are . . . were . . . both friends of Cecily de Vere."

Bauer cleared his throat. After a few moments of thinking, he nodded.

"Yes, well, good," he said. "I have questions." He looked at Rosalind. "Why was your friend on the train? What was her reason for traveling?"

It was such an absurd thing to ask that Rosalind was almost speechless. "She was on the train because she was going to America."

"She is English," Bauer said. "Why would someone from England take a German train when the English have so many ships, hmm? Answer that."

"She came because I invited her," Rosalind said.

"And *you*?" Bauer demanded. "Why did you come? What was your purpose in taking a German train?"

"It's an American train," Rosalind snapped, with more hostility than she had intended. Bauer's tone, combined with the shock and stress, was making her blood boil. "It just happens to leave from Germany."

Bauer frowned. "So you are American?" he asked. "And why were you in Europe?"

"I was visiting my . . . friend," Rosalind said. "Cecily. Her." She blinked a few times to force away the tears that were forming in her eyes. The full realization of Cecily's death was beginning to descend upon her. "I was staying with her family in London . . ."

"In London? Why would you travel from London to Hamburg to go to America? Hmm? Why not leave from England? It is suspicious."

"Suspicious!" Rosalind cried.

"You and your English friend travel to Germany simply

to take the Transatlantic Express?" Bauer said. He shook his head. "No, it is too unlikely. There must be a reason for it." He took a step toward Rosalind, looking her up and down, his face creased in authoritarian anger. "So what is that reason?"

"Because her father owns the railway," Alix said. She withdrew from Rosalind's embrace and stood. "Do you understand now?"

"Her father?" Bauer asked. He backed away from Alix and gave Rosalind a puzzled look. "Your father is—"

"My father is Alexander Wallace," Rosalind admitted, her voice taut and hoarse. Strange: in her bewilderment and grief, she had not even considered telling him who she was. Then again, nothing he'd done had made sense, so perhaps it wouldn't have made a difference. She couldn't understand why he was more intent on making her and Alix feel guilty than he was upset that their friend had been murdered. "You know, the man who built all of this," she added.

Bauer took another step back. The color drained away from his face. He swallowed and set his expression, this time stony with professional detachment rather than openly hostile.

"Miss Wallace. Forgive me. I did not realize who you were."

"I hardly see what difference it makes," Rosalind said. "It shouldn't matter whether we're proper ladies or . . . or fishmongers' daughters! I want to know who killed my friend!"

Bauer held up his hands. He tried to look comforting,

but it was a wasted effort. The twitch in his cheek betrayed his enraged frustration. He'd wanted to break Rosalind, and now he was suddenly forced to show subservience. "We are already looking into it," he said. "We will find whoever is responsible, I give you my word. But in the meantime, you must be honest with me. Can you think of any reason . . . any reason at all . . . why a person might want to harm her?"

Rosalind exchanged a look with Alix. The very suggestion of it was absurd. A motive to kill Cecily? Cecily, of all people . . .

"No, of course not," she said.

"Cecily is . . . was a kind, gentle person," Alix offered. "No one who knew her would want to hurt her, I am sure of it." But then she turned to Rosalind and asked, "What about that man this afternoon?"

Before Rosalind could reply, Bauer stepped toward them again.

"What man?" he demanded.

Rosalind chewed her lip. Given that Cecily's murder made no sense to begin with, she supposed anything was possible. "There was a man who followed us when we took a walk around the station earlier today," she explained to Bauer. "We confronted him . . . and he ran off."

"Who was he?" Bauer asked. "Did you know him?"

"No," Rosalind said. She shook her head vigorously. "None of us recognized him."

"Describe him to me," Bauer said.

"Um . . ." Rosalind thought for a moment. "Six feet tall, I think. No, shorter. Midthirties. Or maybe older. Dark hair. Small mustache. Brown suit and . . . and a bowler hat, if I remember."

Alix nodded. "Yes, a bowler hat. I remember it. And the suit was very common. I think he was a tradesman."

"He's a Second Class passenger," Rosalind said. "I saw him return to a Second Class car on the train."

Bauer looked away, apparently deep in thought. He slowly nodded a few times and muttered something to himself in German. Rosalind could not make out what he was saying.

"Very good," he finally said. He bowed his head, formal and curt. "Ladies, I thank you for your time. We will sort the matter out, have no fear. In the meantime, I suggest that you remain in your compartments for the remainder of the evening."

Rosalind nodded, as did Alix. "Yes, of course," she said, almost mechanically. "Thank you, Inspector."

Bauer motioned to the door. "My men will escort the two of you," he said. "For your safety."

Rosalind took Alix by the arm and went to the door. She looked back over her shoulder at Bauer and said, "You will find the person responsible, Inspector. Won't you?"

"You may trust in me, Miss Wallace," Bauer said.

◊   ◊   ◊

At Rosalind's compartment, under the watchful eyes of Inspector Bauer's men, Alix embraced her tightly. Rosalind hugged her back for a long while. It was so strange that they had met only the day before. Alix was suddenly both her only friend—if one could even call her that—and a terrible reminder of their friend's death, and would be for the duration of the journey. She could almost assume that Alix felt the same way. And how would they get word to Charles, to Cecily's parents? Would the Exham de Veres hold her accountable the way Inspector Bauer had?

"I will call on you tomorrow," Alix said softly, stepping back.

"Thank you," Rosalind said. "Try to get some sleep."

"You, too, Rose."

Rosalind closed the door on Bauer's men, leaning against it with her eyes closed. She took a deep breath and felt the coiled knot of anguish inside her come undone. Only then did she bury her face in her hands and weep.

Rosalind did not recall falling asleep, though this was perhaps for the best. She had lain awake for hours, listening to the sound of the train resuming its journey sometime after midnight. But now she awoke to the sound of someone knocking loudly on the door. She sat upright with a start and looked toward the window. Even at this depth, she could tell by the light filtering down through the ocean that it was daytime.

"Rosalind?" Alix called from the other side of the door. "Rosalind, can you hear me?" Her voice was very faint. The compartment doors were heavy. No wonder the commotion of Cecily and Doris's murder had gone unnoticed.

"Just a moment," Rosalind called. She sat on the edge of the bed and steadied her feet on the floor before standing. Her entire body ached from fatigue. Wiping her raw eyes and cheeks,

Chapter Eleven

Rosalind shot a quick glance at herself in the closest mirror. She was an utter mess. Her hair was disheveled and her clothes—the same ones she'd worn to the ball—were rumpled and misshapen. So when she slid the door open, she was surprised at how bright and fresh Alix appeared: a new dress and not a hair out of place.

"Rosalind," she said, her face twisted in concern, "I did not wake you, did I?"

"Don't worry about it." Rosalind took Alix by the hand and led her into the room. She smiled as best she could manage. "You look . . . tidy."

"Well, we must put on our brave faces, yes?" Alix said.

"My face doesn't feel very brave today."

"Nor mine," Alix agreed. "But we must try. It will not do for us to be seen so upset when we are out in public. People would talk, more than they already will. And we cannot have gossiping about . . . about Cecily."

Rosalind nodded.

"I suppose," she said. "Though truly, I think I would prefer to stay here the entire trip."

"I would as well," Alix said, her voice tinged with the same emotion that Rosalind felt. "But we cannot. It is not what Cecily would want. Now then," she said, "why don't you wash and dress, and I will get us some food."

"I'm not all that hungry . . ." Rosalind began.

"Nor I," Alix said. "But still, we must eat. Neither of us has had anything since last night. And that is not at all good for us. Starving will not bring Cecily back, nor will it find her killer."

"I suppose you're right," Rosalind agreed.

Before she could say anything more, there was another knock at the door, this time a loud pounding, far less subtle than Alix's.

"What now?" Rosalind wondered aloud, though she could guess. As suspected, she opened the door on Inspector Bauer. He stood in the corridor, hands behind his back, his face as dour as it had been the night before.

"Good morning, Miss Wallace." His tone was gruff.

"Good morning, Inspector," Rosalind replied. Though her words were cordial, she could not conceal the tone of *What do you want?* in her voice.

"May I enter?" Bauer asked, motioning to the cabin.

Rosalind frowned. "It would be highly irregular for me to allow strange men into my private rooms," she said.

Bauer smiled and said, "You needn't worry. I am with the police."

"So I recall."

"The police your father invited aboard," he clarified.

After a moment's thought, Rosalind stepped aside. The sooner he concluded his business, the sooner he would leave her alone.

Bauer entered and closed the door behind him, but he remained just inside the threshold, keeping his distance. At least he had that much decency. "I have news regarding your poor departed friend," he said.

"You do?" Alix cried.

"We have the murderer in custody," Bauer said grimly.

Rosalind shook her head a few times, wondering if she had heard correctly. "You . . . what?" she asked.

"We have the man," Bauer said, meeting her stare.

"So quickly? How?" Rosalind wanted to feel relieved at the knowledge, but the swiftness of Bauer's victory made her uneasy. It was too simple a thing. One night, and he had solved this terrible crime? Rosalind couldn't accept that . . . until she reminded herself where they were. They were trapped under the sea; they were sealed off from the world. There were only a hundred passengers, and an equal number of crew members—and that meant there were only some two hundred possible suspects, most of whom could be dismissed immediately. No wonder he'd been so rude in his interrogation last night.

"You speak as if you doubt the capabilities of the Hamburg Police," Bauer said, not masking his offense. "We are very capable investigators, Miss Wallace. And it was not a difficult case."

"Who was responsible?" Alix asked hesitantly.

Bauer reached into his coat pocket and withdrew a photograph. It was still damp, clearly developed within the past hour. He held it out to Rosalind for inspection. Though the image was a bit blurry, Rosalind spotted the mustache immediately.

"Do you recognize this man?" Bauer asked.

"Yes, of course," Rosalind said. "He's the man from yesterday."

"The one who was watching us," Alix added.

Bauer nodded. "As I thought. Rest assured he's in safe custody. Once we arrive in America, he will be dealt with."

"What makes you so sure it was him?" Rosalind asked as Bauer turned to leave, tucking the photo back into his coat pocket.

He scowled over his shoulder. "I deliver you the man, and now you question his guilt?" he asked. "Did you not tell me yourself that he stalked you and your friend yesterday?"

"I apologize," Rosalind said, keeping her voice steady. "And I am certainly pleased that he is under arrest, but that still doesn't mean he committed the murder. I don't want the guilty person going free just because this man is more convenient."

Bauer snorted. "I understand your thinking," he said. "Why would someone murder an innocent young aristocrat? But have no doubt, Miss Wallace: we have the right man. It was robbery. He broke into your friend's room, killed her, and stole her jewels. He's a butcher from Bremen traveling on a Second Class ticket. He attempted to sneak into First Class yesterday. We reprimanded him and sent a cable back to the authorities to investigate, but learned too late that he is a thief who wishes to advantage himself at the expense of his betters. He will be punished for it. Do not fear."

Rosalind glanced at Alix, who'd collapsed on Rosalind's bed. Alix's head was in her hands. She was shaking with silent sobs. The story was becoming more far-fetched by the minute. But there was no point in arguing. Bauer wanted her to accept what he was saying. Why, she could not fathom, but everything told her that she was expected to agree with him and then leave well enough alone.

She nodded slowly. "Of course, Inspector. As I think about it, it all makes a great deal of sense. Please do forgive me for being skeptical. I'm not really myself at the moment. You understand."

This seemed to placate him. Bauer smiled at her like a strict headmaster indulging an apologetic child. "I think under the circumstances you may be forgiven for such a lapse in judgment. You are grieving. Possibly hysterical."

"Utterly hysterical," Rosalind replied flatly. "Thank you for informing me of these developments, Inspector. I am . . ." She glanced at Alix. "We are most grateful to you for having caught that horrible man before he hurt anyone else. Now if you wouldn't mind . . ." She nodded toward the door.

"Of course," Bauer said. "And I need not tell you that it would be best not to speak of this to anyone on the train. Anyone. Gossip can be very dangerous. We do not want anyone to panic unnecessarily, thinking that they may be in danger. You understand, of course. And so you know, we have placed both bodies on ice. When we reach New York City, arrangements will be made to have them returned to England."

A lump lodged itself in Rosalind's throat, making it very difficult for her to speak. He spoke of Cecily and Doris as if they'd been fish caught to bring to market. "Very sensible," she managed, but her voice was strained. "Again, our thanks. But now I fear that I must ask you to leave."

Bauer nodded. He reached for the door handle.

"Your friend had a brother, I believe," he said, pausing.

Rosalind felt her heartbeat quicken at the mention of Charles. How did Bauer know that? And why was he interested?

"Yes, she did," she replied, keeping her voice calm. "Why?"

"Curiosity," Bauer said. "And I believe I read that he was to join you on the journey."

"Yes, the papers did say that," Rosalind answered. *Hadn't they?*

"And did he? Is he with you on the train?"

What an absurd question, Rosalind thought. Aloud, she replied, "No, he certainly did not. And I've been dreading to think how he will take this news. No doubt he will blame himself for not coming with us."

Bauer grunted. "Well, then. Thank you for your time and for your discretion. I am sorry for your loss. Good day, Fräulein Wallace."

"Good day, Inspector," Rosalind replied.

Only after the door had closed behind him and the faint sound of his footsteps had faded did Rosalind shriek with frustration. She clenched her hands into fists. Until now, she had been overwhelmed with sorrow. Now that sorrow had been replaced with rage. She paced the room furiously.

"What is it, Rosalind?" Alix asked from the bed, a little hesitantly.

"Alix, may I be candid with you?" Rosalind asked.

"Of course," Alix said. "Cecily was my dear friend, as she was yours. I would like to believe that you can speak to me as you would to her . . ." Alix looked up at Rosalind and suddenly she seemed so very lost and forlorn, afraid and alone. Rosalind knew exactly how she felt. They were *both* outsiders now. Cecily had been the strongest source of companionship for both of them, and now she was gone.

Without thinking, Rosalind rushed to the bed and hugged Alix tightly. Alix clung to her, sobbing softly into her shoulder. After a few moments, Rosalind withdrew.

"I am . . . I am sorry," Alix said, wiping her eyes with her fingertips. She took a handkerchief from her sleeve and dabbed at her face in an effort to undo the damage. "I thought I was more composed than this."

Rosalind placed her hands on Alix's shoulders and tried her best to smile reassuringly. "Don't apologize," she said. "You are upset. I am upset. And we have a right to be."

Alix nodded a little. "So, what do you wish to be candid about?" she said hoarsely.

"About Cecily's death," Rosalind said. "Alix, I am quite certain that the police have the wrong man."

"What?" Alix gasped.

"Or even if he is the right one, they have no idea of his actual motive."

"You don't believe it was robbery?" Alix asked.

Rosalind shook her head. "No," she said, "it wasn't robbery. Cecily's jewels were still all there on the table. I remember seeing them. Not much of a robbery if nothing's stolen, is it?"

"I suppose not," Alix said softly. "Perhaps he was too afraid to take anything?"

"Too afraid to steal but courageous enough to kill?" Rosalind countered. "Perhaps, but I don't think so. Why didn't he just flee the moment he realized there were people in the room? Lord knows, he'd probably have gotten away unidentified."

"But . . . a thief . . . a criminal . . . Would such a man be thinking clearly?" Alix stammered.

"I don't think such a man would have broken into the room at all," Rosalind replied. "A butcher trying to sneak into First Class? And then robbing the rich to feed his criminal inclinations? I think Inspector Bauer has a rather dim view of the lower classes, Alix."

Rosalind stood again and resumed pacing back and forth. She often did this when agitated; it was yet another one of those dreadful habits Mother always reminded her about when company came to visit. But if Alix were irritated or took offense, she gave no indication. Instead she sat on the edge of the bed, her hands folded in her lap, attentive.

"The man did not seem like he had good intentions when we first encountered him," Alix pointed out. "You yourself were frightened."

"I agree; he seemed dreadful. But he also seemed like an abject coward. Unnerved when confronted by the three girls he was following? Erich and Jacob's arrival may have confirmed it, but he was ready to run before that. I think that hatpin was what did the trick."

Alix managed a sad smile. "It's a good hatpin," she said.

"Right, but I can't imagine he would break into someone's compartment and then kill two people upon discovery," Rosalind said. "So either it wasn't him, or else he had quite a different purpose than theft."

"And also, I suppose now would be a foolish time to stage a robbery," Alix noted.

Rosalind paused and stood still. "How do you mean?"

"Well . . . the second day of the journey?" Alix shook her head. "If the man were a thief, if he had more courage and cleverness than we are giving him credit for, then he would also have better sense. He'd wait until the last day. Wait until we are pulling into the station. The police might never catch him then. But if he committed a crime last night? The entire train would be in an uproar over the theft. Baggage searched, rooms examined."

Rosalind nodded slowly. Alix was absolutely right about that. "He would have no place to run to," she said. "A whole week left before landfall. He'd be discovered for sure. What could he have been thinking? That he would escape in a submarine? It's ridiculous."

Alix looked down at her hands, her lips twisting into a narrow frown. After a while, she looked up at Rosalind. "So you think Cecily was killed . . . for another reason?"

Rosalind nodded. She disliked the very notion, but there it was. "As unthinkable as it is, it's far more plausible than the idea that someone would kill her simply for the sake of robbing her when they had no hope of escape for five days."

"Who would want to do such a thing?" Alix asked. "And why? Cecily was the kindest, gentlest person in the world."

"I know," Rosalind said. "Mistaken identity, perhaps? Someone else was the intended victim, but the killer got the wrong room?"

"But as with robbery, why not wait until the end of the journey?" Alix asked.

"I . . . I don't know." Rosalind sighed and pressed her palms against her temples. This was going to get them nowhere, and in the meantime she would drive herself mad with questions and uncertainty. "There must be a reason."

Alix stood and quickly took Rosalind's hands in hers. "We *will* find the answer. Please don't do yourself harm trying to unravel it all."

Rosalind took a few deep breaths and nodded. "Of course."

"Now, I am going to reserve a table for some late breakfast," Alix said. "I think it is very important that you and I try to act as normal as possible while we are trapped down here, yes?"

"Yes, you are right, Alix," Rosalind agreed, taking another deep breath. "Normalcy. We should set a routine and follow it. Though I don't know how much I can bear being around people."

"We will try a little bit at a time, *ja?*" Alix said. "I do hope that I am not included in 'people.'" She looked away, the cloud of sorrow again haunting her face. "I don't think I want to be alone right now."

Rosalind reached out to give Alix's hand a firm squeeze. "You're certainly not 'people,' Alix," she said. "You're a friend. And while I don't think I can bear a crowd for very long, I don't want to be alone, either."

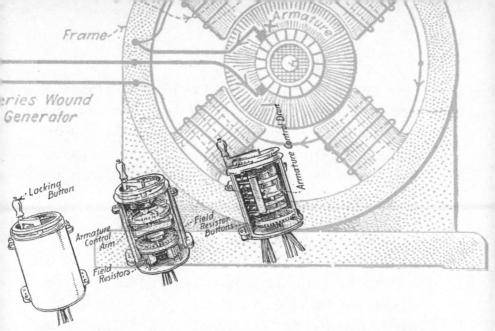

Frame

Armature

ries Wound
Generator

Armature Control Drum

Locking
Button

Armature
Control
Arm

Field
Resistor
Buttons

Field
Resistors

While Rosalind was relieved to spend the day entirely in Alix's company, she couldn't help but dwell on dark thoughts, regrets, and guilt. She found herself reliving the events of the previous night, questioning whether Cecily's murder had been avoidable. If it was somehow her fault. If she had only gone to check on her friend . . . If she had only stopped by on her way to the ball . . . If she had only . . .

After eating, they ensconced themselves in a corner of the Red Parlor. As they settled into the plush armchairs, the speakers in the room crackled to life with a loud whistle. Rosalind immediately tensed. She exchanged a nervous look with Alix. Was the captain going to mention what had happened? Surely, no . . . A double murder would be cause to panic.

As always, the captain's tinny announcement

came first in German and then in English. "Good day, ladies and gentlemen. This is your captain speaking. We hope that you are enjoying your journey after last night's festivities. Today we are entirely at sea and tomorrow we will stop for the evening at the Neptune Station, in the middle of the Atlantic."

Rosalind sighed. "Just when I thought that a walk might do me some good," she joked grimly.

"You sound like Cecily," Alix said. She chuckled softly, but then the two of them looked away and fell silent. The captain was babbling in German again. Suddenly Alix started glaring at the nearest speaker. "Of all the . . ." she muttered.

"What is it?" Rosalind asked.

Alix held up a hand for silence. But Rosalind did not have to wait long for her answer, for the captain began repeating the latest portion of his message in English:

"Now, you may have heard some rumors regarding an unfortunate incident that took place onboard the train last night. I shall not go into details. Rest assured that everything is under control and there is no cause for concern. Please disregard any gossip you may hear regarding the matter. I would caution you all against idle speculation. Do not disturb your neighbors with unfounded rumors. Thank you, that is all."

Rosalind felt her cheeks burning with anger. So that was his strategy for quelling panic. She couldn't believe it. Idle speculation? Rumors? Gossip? He'd just engaged in all three. Worse, he was treating Cecily's death like it hadn't even happened.

"They don't want anyone finding out," Alix said.

"Of course they don't," Rosalind hissed. "More to the point, they don't want all the passengers demanding that they reverse course, return to Hamburg, and give them their money back."

"I suppose they would." Alix nodded with understanding.

"I certainly would," Rosalind said.

"Shouldn't we tell someone?" Alix asked. "People deserve to know."

Rosalind nodded, looking off across the room. Her eyes came to rest on a man reading a newspaper at one of the nearby tables. He glanced in her direction, but when he realized that he had been seen, he quickly buried his nose back in his paper. But Rosalind recognized him. He had been with Bauer the night before. And he had been in the library car that first evening, pretending to be the librarian. Only he wasn't a librarian. He was one of Bauer's henchmen.

Lowering her voice, she said to Alix, "You see that man there?" She nodded slightly in his direction with her head.

"Yes," Alix answered, sounding very confused. "Why?"

"I think he works for Inspector Bauer," Rosalind said. "He was the one who raced after him in the dining car our first night aboard."

Alix's eyes became as wide as saucers. She huddled back into her chair, suddenly afraid.

"You don't think he's . . . he's spying on us, do you?"

"I'm certain of it," Rosalind replied. "I think Bauer is having us watched, to be sure we don't tell anyone about what happened."

The sense of panic was even stronger now. Rosalind gripped the armrests of her chair in an effort to steady herself. *Bauer is just taking precautions. He doesn't want a panic*, she reminded herself. Father wouldn't have wanted a panic, either. They were young, and they were female, and so Bauer didn't trust their discretion. It was that simple.

Rosalind rose to her feet and grabbed Alix's hand. "Come along," she said, "let's get some fresh air."

                        ✿   ✿   ✿

The race to the arboreal car, while tugging Alix along behind her, felt rather like a dream—or more accurately, a nightmare. Rosalind kept looking over her shoulder to be sure Bauer's man was not following them, though there were so many nondescript men in suits about that it was impossible to determine which of them might be with the police. The only real clue she could think of was that a policeman could not afford the expensive clothes of a gentleman, so she kept alert for any men in First Class wearing cheap, drab suits.

"Rosalind, please go slower," Alix begged. "You are hurting my arm."

"Oh . . ." Rosalind said, pausing to turn. "I'm so sorry . . ." Her voice died when she saw one of the porters moving down the corridor behind them, carrying an armload of boxes. His mouth was concealed behind his burden, but Rosalind could see his eyes. Was he following them? Was *he* one of Bauer's men as well?

"My, you're in a hurry, Fräulein Wallace," a voice said.

"Oh, my goodness!" she exclaimed. She whirled around and almost slammed into Erich. He was alone. "Herr Steiner! I am so very sorry!"

Erich looked perplexed, but he kept smiling. "Good afternoon," he said, straightening his tie. He glanced at Alix and gave her a polite nod. "And hello to you, Lady von Hessen. Fancy meeting the two of you here."

"In the corridor?" Alix asked.

"It doesn't seem all that far-fetched," Rosalind agreed.

"No, no," he said with a short laugh. He furrowed his brow. "What I mean is that Jacob and I were very concerned when you disappeared last night. We were afraid we may have done something to offend you."

"Oh. Oh, goodness, no—" Rosalind's throat caught. "It's just . . . Well, it's complicated."

"I can only imagine," Erich said. "To have missed such a wonderful ball, you must have had something important to attend to. But it is amusing, because I have spent all day looking for you to apologize and to inquire what might be the problem. And now here you are."

Rosalind swallowed, willing herself not to cry. "I assure you, our disappearance last night is nothing to do with you."

"I am relieved to hear it," Erich said genially, either not noticing their distress or pretending not to. "And Jacob will be relieved as well."

"We're just going to the . . ." Rosalind began.

"Yes?" Erich asked, a little too eagerly.

"We're just going to the arboreal car," she finished.

"Oh, what a coincidence," Erich said. "I was thinking of going there, too. May I join you?"

"Well, um . . ." Rosalind stammered.

"Say yes," Alix breathed in her ear.

Rosalind laughed awkwardly. But she rallied and gave Erich a nod.

"Your company would be much appreciated, Herr Steiner," she said.

Oh, God, why did everything in life have to be so confusing?

❂   ❂   ❂

By the time he'd led the way to the arboretum, she'd reined in her muddled thoughts. The rush of fresh air was a welcome relief, despite the crowd of First Class passengers who'd clearly had the same idea. Spotting an empty clearing with a pair of wrought-iron benches, Rosalind slumped into one of them, grateful to be off her unsteady feet. Alix sat beside her.

"Now then, what became of you two last night?" Erich asked as he seated himself on the bench across from them.

"Umm . . ." Rosalind said. "I am terribly sorry, Herr Steiner—"

"I would prefer that you called me Erich."

After a little hesitation, Rosalind nodded. "If you insist, Erich."

"I do, Fräulein Wallace," Erich said, his eyes twinkling.

"If I am going to call you by your Christian name," Rosalind said, "presumably you ought to do the same. Erich."

"As you like, Rose—"

"You may continue to call me Lady von Hessen," Alix interrupted.

Erich blinked, but his smile didn't waver. "As you wish, my lady. Now then, last night . . ."

"I am sorry," Rosalind said, "but I really don't wish to speak about it."

He leaned forward, his expression one of deep concern. "Yes, of course, as you like," he said. "Never let it be said that I am a man who intrudes upon a lady's private affairs."

"Thank you," Rosalind said. "It is appreciated."

"But of course," Erich told her. "Mmm, tell me though, did you hear that announcement from the captain a few minutes ago?"

Alix fidgeted beside her. Rosalind started to feel queasy. "We did, yes," she answered.

"I do not want you to think me a gossip," Erich said, lowering his voice, "but I have a tidbit to share about that."

Rosalind leaned back against the cold metal of the bench. This was awkward. Yes, she was curious about what Erich might think he knew, but under no circumstances did she want to be caught discussing it.

"Oh?" Alix asked in the silence, her tone both demanding and skeptical. In that one word she had summed up Rosalind's true feelings on the matter.

Erich slid forward in his seat. "I heard that there was a robbery last night," he whispered. "Can you believe it?"

Rosalind stopped breathing.

"No," Alix said dully. "You can't be serious."

Was that sarcasm? Rosalind eyed her. Why was Alix

playing along? That would be a horrid thing to do, wouldn't it, knowing what they knew? But perhaps it was simply her way of managing her grief. Or it might be more than that: a shrewd effort not to draw attention to themselves and their loss.

"Of course, there is no need to fear," Erich said quickly, straightening his posture. "I understand that they caught the man. Some Second Class passenger. People these days, you know. You cannot trust anyone, can you?"

"So it seems," Alix agreed softly. She stared down at her lap.

"Erich," Rosalind said, "how did you come to hear about this? Who told you?"

Erich seemed surprised. "No one told me," he replied. "Well, Jacob did. He overheard it at breakfast. I thought you might be interested. It's exciting . . . isn't it?"

Rosalind wanted to scream. Exciting? No, that would not be her word of choice to describe last night's horror. But it seemed Erich was simply trying to impress her with some idle gossip. The captain's strategy had been tailor-made to backfire; she could imagine *everyone* on the train gossiping now. Still, if Erich and Jacob had found out about Bauer's inane theory regarding the botched robbery, who might be spreading the rumors? No wonder Bauer's men were stalking her: they probably suspected that she and Alix were the source. The situation was staggering in its irony.

Alix's mouth twisted into a frown. She stood. "I think . . ." she began. "I think I am going to find Jacob and have a few words with him."

"Not on my account, I hope," Erich said breezily. "It's just a rumor, you know. Though I am certain Jacob would be glad to see you."

Alix nodded. She placed a hand on Rosalind's shoulder. "If I do not see you before this evening," she said, "dinner?"

"Yes, of course," Rosalind agreed.

With that, Alix gave Erich another polite nod. But as she left, she said something in German that made him raise his eyebrows.

"What did she say to you?" Rosalind asked once Alix had vanished in the direction of the sleeper cars.

Erich snickered. "She said that she would leave you in my care, and that she expected me to behave as an absolute gentleman. On pain of death by hatpin."

That made Rosalind smile, if only briefly.

"I don't know what good talking to Jacob will do," Erich continued. "He just overheard some idle chat at breakfast."

"Perhaps," Rosalind agreed, "but I suspect she will feel better for it."

"There's no danger," Erich reassured her.

Rosalind opened her mouth, but no words would come. She wanted to play along now, too, as Alix had. She wanted so desperately to agree with Erich. But the lump in her throat swelled once more. A tear fell from her cheek. She brushed it aside and sniffed, staring straight at him. "Erich, Cecily was murdered last night."

The color drained from his face. "This is a joke."

She shook her head and swallowed. "It is no joke. Alix and I found her. That is why we vanished last night."

"Cecily dead . . ." Erich put his hand over his mouth and leaned back against the bench, shaking his head. "My God, my God. And the maid?"

Rosalind raised an eyebrow. "Her maid was murdered as well, yes . . ."

"Murdered?" Erich exclaimed. "I meant has someone told her. Both of them were murdered? Oh my God. That poor girl." He lunged forward and grabbed Rosalind's hand, holding it firmly. Looking into her eyes, he said, "Rosalind, I do not know what to say. But I am so very sorry for your loss. If there were any way I could undo this for you, I would make it happen."

Rosalind tried to answer, but her face twisted and she felt the tears coming again. Erich let go and drew a handkerchief from his pocket. He pressed it into her palm. Rosalind nodded, grateful, and dabbed at her eyes.

"Thank you," she whispered.

Erich stood. "I simply cannot believe it. Cecily was killed by that . . . that ruffian?" He looked at her again, his jaw tight. "But they caught the man. At least there is that. At least there will be justice."

Rosalind looked into Erich's eyes. She fought the urge to tell him everything: about her suspicions, about the absurdity of the whole situation, that she felt certain they had the wrong man, certain that there was something more than robbery behind it all. But there was no point in drawing him into a nightmare about which she herself knew nothing. Instead, she forced a weak smile and passed the handkerchief back to him.

"Rosalind," Erich said.

"Yes?"

"Tomorrow we stop for the day at Neptune Station. I wonder . . ."

"Yes?"

Erich hesitated. "There is to be another ball. Now, of course, under the circumstances, I do not expect you feel much like dancing."

"No, not really," Rosalind said, smiling through her tears.

"No, of course not," he murmured. "However, should you decide that a dance might cheer you up, I would be honored if it would be with me." He held up a hand. "But that is not what I want to ask. I wondered if . . . before lunch tomorrow, if you might . . ."

"Yes . . . ?"

"Would you perhaps care to take a walk with me, when we reach Neptune Station tomorrow?" Erich asked. "Just the two of us, or perhaps with Jacob and Lady von Hessen? Just for an hour or two. I confess that I enjoy your company, what little of it I have been privileged to, and I would like to think that I might help ease your pain."

Rosalind closed her eyes. After a little while, she nodded. "I think that would be most agreeable, Herr . . . Erich. Thank you for your kindness. Now, if you will excuse me, I would like to be alone for a little while."

Erich bowed to her as she stood. "Yes, of course," he said. "But if you have need of me, please do not hesitate to seek me out."

"I am grateful of that," Rosalind said. Then she hurried

to the edge of the clearing, back toward the path to the exit.

"Rosalind," Erich called after her.

She turned back to look at him. His eyes were glistening, as if her tears had become contagious.

"I am . . . I am very sorry for what has happened to you," he said. "You have all of my sympathy."

"Thank you," she said. Before she could start crying again, she ran.

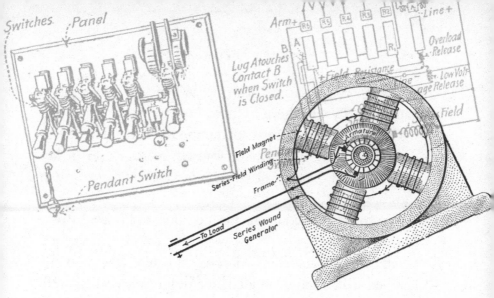

Rosalind requested that Alix join her for dinner in her compartment rather than in the dining carriages. She couldn't bear the thought of eating amid the crowd, especially when the other passengers knew nothing of her sorrow, when her presence would reduce what little was known to grotesque innuendo. Imagine, the murdered girl traveling in the company of the railway owner's daughter! Surely that could not be a coincidence, the gossips would reason. Cecily deserved better than idle talk or cold disinterest, her own penchant for gossip aside. Rosalind did not care to be around people who had no respect for the victims of crimes.

In the dark silence of the meal, however, Rosalind realized that she had not really appreciated how Cecily's fondness for prattle and nonsense had kept conversation flowing. Whenever there was a pause, Cecily was there to fill it. No longer.

Over the main course of lamb, Rosalind decided to do what Cecily would have wanted, to carry on in her absence. And that meant talking, not merely drowning in the clattering of silverware.

"So you're related to the Grand Duke of Hesse?" Rosalind asked.

Alix looked up from her food, startled. But then she laughed a little and nodded, seemingly pleased as well. "Yes," she said. "We are cousins somewhere along the line. I forget how many places removed and that sort of thing. But we visit often. It is rather nice." She took another nibble of her lamb. "You know, the empress of Russia is another cousin of mine."

"Really?" Rosalind asked, though she was not surprised. The aristocracy of Europe was so interconnected that she'd grown accustomed to such coincidences.

Alix nodded. "People think that I am named for her, but I'm not."

"Who are you named for, then?"

"I don't know, actually," Alix said. She shrugged. "Hmm. I never asked. Isn't that silly of me?"

"Not at all," Rosalind answered. "I've never asked why I'm called Rosalind."

"Because it is a pretty name," Alix said. "I like it."

"Thank you," Rosalind said, blushing a little at the compliment. "Evidently my mother liked it as well. And Cecily liked it most of all."

Alix put her silverware down. "Cecily liked your name

very much. She repeated it often. 'Rose this' and 'Rose that.' She was very fond of you. At school she would go on and on about Rose, her dear friend Rose. Like you were her big sister."

Rosalind's throat tightened. Her eyes began to sting. She drew in a quivering breath, staring at her plate, and then dropped her own silver. "I can't imagine why," she managed. "We had only seen each other half a dozen times then. It wasn't until this year that we spent any proper time together . . ."

Alix reached out and took Rosalind's hand. "I think, perhaps, she needed someone to look up to. Someone *like* a sister." She let go and settled back into her chair. "How did you and Cecily come to know each other? It seems so strange, being friends across the ocean like that. I mean, if you aren't related."

"It was our fathers," Rosalind said. "Back . . . um . . . ten years ago, I think . . . My father had just partnered with the German government to build the railway. That had been a dreadful year. He'd dragged us all across Europe trying to sell the idea. And no one wanted to buy it. They always would say, 'We have ships, why do we need a train?'"

"How unprogressive of them," Alix said, digging back into her food.

Rosalind nodded, relieved to have a sympathetic ear about such matters, which she'd never discussed—not even with Cecily. "After the Germans came round, Lord Exham wrote a letter to my father congratulating him on the whole enterprise. He was shocked that the British hadn't taken him up on it, and he was very keen to become an investor and all that."

Alix looked up. "Goodness," she said.

"Oh, yes, it was quite unexpected," Rosalind said. "Like a bolt from the blue. But it was also rather wonderful. Lord Exham invited my father to join him in building railways in Canada, and then Ireland, and then India, and it just went on from there. Our families became friends, so Cecily and I were expected to become friends. Fortunately, we did."

"It is difficult not to become friends with Cecily," Alix said, her voice catching. "It *was* difficult not to," she corrected herself.

This time, Rosalind reached out. She placed a hand on Alix's arm. She knew exactly how the girl felt. It was so horrid, swinging back and forth from grief to futile attempts at forgetting, and then back to grief. "She will be well remembered," Rosalind said. Her voice hardened. "And avenged, if I have anything to say about it."

Alix nodded. "My thoughts precisely." She shook herself and lifted her fork again. "But enough of such talk. Let us remain happy."

"Yes," Rosalind agreed. "It's what Cecily would have wanted."

"So tell me, Rosalind . . ." Alix said. "I understand that you are a very scandalous person who harbors all manner of unacceptable opinions regarding the world. Would you care to rebut some of these accusations, or are you immensely proud of them?"

Rosalind had to laugh. "Of each and every one of them," she said.

"List them all, if you please," Alix said wryly. "In order categorical."

"I don't even know how one would do that," Rosalind replied.

"Alphabetical?" Alix ventured.

It almost hurt to smile, but it also felt very good. "Well, aside from driving motorcars," Rosalind began, "I speak without being spoken to—"

"How horrible of you," Alix interjected.

"I believe in giving women the vote—"

"Scandalous."

"Home rule for all people everywhere—"

"Even the Alsatians?"

"Especially the Alsatians," Rosalind confirmed. "I am a pacifist, I ride bicycles, and I am a proud member of the Anti-Imperialist League."

"I did not know there was such a thing," Alix said.

Rosalind laughed. "It's true. Mister Carnegie is a member. We are committed to the defense of the American ideal from the corrupting influences of empire." She raised a finger into the air. "We cannot have democracy for some and not for all!"

Across the table, Alix dropped her silver and clapped her hands.

Rosalind's face felt hot. Suddenly she was embarrassed at her own enthusiasm. "You're not making fun of me, are you?" she asked. "I know that I can get carried away at times—"

"Not at all." Alix shook her head. "No, I am very pleased by it." She leaned forward. "So you believe that America should not aspire to be an empire?"

"It would be the death of our ideals," Rosalind answered.

"What about the European empires?" Alix asked.

"They ought to be abolished," Rosalind said. "Nobody should be ruled by a king or emperor half a world away in Europe."

Alix's eyes sparkled, as if she was growing more excited with each word. She leaned forward, on the verge of falling from the edge of her chair. "What do you think about class barriers?"

"I . . ." All at once, Rosalind felt very odd. Alix did seem genuinely interested in her opinions and delighted at her responses, but this made no sense at all. Alix was an aristocrat. Her entire world was built upon privilege and empire. Why would she be happy to hear that Rosalind despised everything her world represented? But even as she posed the question to herself, she could guess the reason: Alix was just desperate for any distraction, any way to avoid dwelling on the death of their friend.

No matter. Honesty above all.

"I despise class barriers and class privilege," Rosalind finished. "And I'm not ashamed to say it. People ought to be judged on their accomplishments, on their conduct and strength of character, not whether their daddy is the third marquis of Such-and-such. And I grow so very tired of Society pooh-poohing self-made men, like there's something wrong with having earned your money."

Alix nodded. "Yes?"

Rosalind hesitated a little bit, again unnerved by Alix's attentiveness. The girl appeared positively riveted, more so now than at any time since they'd met. But she continued: "My grandfather was a self-made man. My father more so, obviously. But my grandfather came over from Scotland with nothing, literally nothing, and he worked hard and built himself up until he was . . . well, not rich, I suppose, but wealthy enough. The fact that he did it on his own should be cause for celebration, not a family secret to be hidden away in a cupboard."

"Your family is ashamed of your grandfather?" Alix pressed.

Yes, Rosalind nearly blurted out. But she caught herself. It was true: no one spoke of her grandfather in public. It was as if they pretended that her father had sprung full-grown from the American soil—without parentage, but with enough respectability (or rather, money) to wed her mother.

"Let's just say we don't speak about him," Rosalind said. "But it turns out all the respectability in the world can't buy food or pay off one's gambling debts." She paused for breath. What was she confessing? And why? The Wallace family secrets weren't Alix's business. No, they were meant to be kept hidden at all times, whatever the cost. Because the family's reputation was so very important. Because Society people were such wonderful company. Because here she was, across from a von Hessen . . .

"Gambling debts?" Alix looked confused.

"My mother's uncle . . ." Rosalind answered hesitantly.

"He has a passion for slow horses." She quickly waved her hands to dismiss the topic. "It's not important."

"No," Alix agreed, "what is important is that you are born to privilege, yet you are angry that your privilege is not shared by all people."

"I suppose so, yes," Rosalind said. She folded her arms and looked away. Then, despite herself, she jumped to her feet and began pacing back and forth. Surely she was making a terrible display and leaving Alix with a horrid impression of her. The girl would likely never speak to her again after that night, and of course Mother and Father would be furious once they inevitably found out what she had been saying.

But dash them, what difference did it make? Cecily was dead, Inspector Bauer's men were following her, and she was tired of it all. Tired of holding her tongue. Tired of worrying about what people might think.

"Think about last night," she said to Alix. "We here in First Class enjoyed lunch and dinner in opulent surroundings, and then we had a ball beneath the sea."

"It was all rather lovely, until . . . until *it* happened," Alix said softly.

"But what about the Second Class passengers?" Rosalind asked. "They'd been cooped up on the train as long as we had, and in much smaller accommodations. Did they enjoy what we enjoyed?"

"No," Alix answered.

Rosalind kept pacing. "That's right, they did not. They took their meals indoors, on the train, just as they did the day before and just as they will for the entire journey. And were they allowed to go to the ball?" She paused. "I suppose you'll tell me these are ghastly things to say."

Alix rose from her chair and folded her hands in front of her chest. "Hardly," she said. "They're not ghastly; they're true. Rosalind, you may not believe me, you certainly won't understand me, but I feel just as you do."

Rosalind raised an eyebrow. "Truly?" she asked.

"As God is my witness," Alix said. "I despise class privilege. I despise empire. They are corruption, Rosalind, and they will be the downfall of us all, just like Rome before us."

"But . . . but . . ." Rosalind stammered.

This was absurd. Cecily's friend from boarding school: a radical? An anti-imperialist? Alix was *nobility*. Rosalind at least could look back to her grandfather's humble origins and find in them a source for her beliefs—however confused those beliefs might be. But a von Hessen?

"You're an aristocrat," she protested. "I don't understand. Why would you oppose everything that your position gives you?"

Alix sniffed. "This asked by the daughter of a rich industrialist and a lady of New York Society?" she mused. "I despise my class for the same reason that you despise yours, Rose. What use is the aristocracy now? We do nothing. We dare not contribute to intellectual discourse, so fearful are we that someone might use it against us to threaten our stature. If you think that your life is stifling, Rosalind, you must try mine." She paused. "Though perhaps our experiences are not all that different."

Rosalind sighed and sank back into her chair. "The

gilded cage is still a cage. Oh, but look at me. Who am I
to speak of such things? And how dare I speak of injus-
tice when I still happily go to balls and spend my father's
money and cross the Atlantic on his train?"

Alix circled the table to join Rosalind. "That is foolish
talk," she snapped. "What matters is not how you were
born, but what you do. You said that yourself. It is true for
the rich as well as for the lowly. You and I were not born
poor. Lamenting our wealth is self-righteous martyrdom.
It serves nothing, do you understand me?"

Rosalind looked at Alix, unsure of how to respond. In
truth, she did not understand a thing about this girl.

"You care about people, Rose," Alix added. "About
people. All people. That is the first step. Next, you must
act."

"Act?" Rosalind repeated.

Alix blinked. Perhaps she realized how dramatic she
had become, for she backed away and stood by her chair.
"I . . . I'm sorry, Rose." She stumbled over her words. "I
didn't mean to get so philosophical. I'm just in a state over
. . . what happened. I should go. It is growing late and I
am tired."

"What?" Rose stood. "But—"

"Please." Alix stepped forward. Then she hesitated and
drew away again. "I think we should speak no more about
such things while we are traveling. I got carried away.
Perhaps when we arrive in New York City, there will be
an opportunity for more such . . . conversations."

Rosalind shook her head. She was almost tempted to
block Alix's exit. "Alix, I don't understand . . ." *She* had

been the one going on about madcap ideas, not Alix. She was grateful for a sympathetic ear. She should be the one worried about speaking out of turn. What the devil was going on?

"I must go," Alix insisted. She hurried toward the door. "But know this, Rosalind. You are not alone in your thoughts. There are many who wish to make the world a better place." She gave Rosalind a last look and smiled. Then she was gone, sliding the door shut behind her.

Rosalind stood still for a very long time. Then she glanced down at the half-finished dinner.

"What did I say?" she wondered aloud.

Switches. Panel

Resistance. Blow-out Coil Line

Line +

Arm. Overload Release

B A Line - Low Voltage Release

Lug A touches Contact B when Switch is Closed. +Field Resistance

Shunt Field Series Field

Arma- ture

Pendant Switch

Pendant Switch Ventilating Holes

Ventilating Duct

Ventilating Air Intake

The Transatlantic Express arrived at Neptune Station ahead of schedule, shortly after breakfast—and Rosalind hadn't seen a soul apart from a member of the waitstaff. He hadn't said anything to her, of course, other than what was required of manners; he'd simply cleared her dinner and brought her the first meal of the day: tea, fresh bread, butter, jam, a sausage. She'd eaten alone in her room—in a daze, her mind whirling as the train slowed toward its next stop.

On the one hand, it was marvelous to learn that she was *not* alone, neither on the train nor in her political or philosophical views. But on the other hand, Alix's behavior disturbed her. It couldn't have been just a way to deflect their attention from the loss of their friend. Perhaps it was the excitement of meeting a like-minded person. She couldn't have met many, after all.

Rosalind hoped that today Alix would be more herself. Then again, how could she be, under the circumstances? Besides, Rosalind didn't really know the girl. Maybe Alix was capricious like this; maybe it took the trauma of Cecily's death to reveal her true personality.

It was best not to think about what she didn't know, Rosalind decided as she stepped off the train into Neptune Station.

The place was much like the Brandenburg in terms of its layout. It had the same vaulted glass ceiling, providing a splendid view of the surrounding sea; the same polished brass and marble; the balconies, sitting rooms, and all the rest. But here, to her relief, there was no hint of nationalism. This was a grand homage to the wonders of the sea. The statues and tapestries were of mermaids and fish rather than of eagles and . . . well, more eagles.

As one of the first passengers to disembark, Rosalind was able to stroll about the concourse in solitude. Erich would be joining her soon enough for their appointed stroll. The few others were from Second Class, probably used to rising earlier. Rosalind did not mind the sparse crowd. She could imagine Cecily gawking at the statues of mermaids, delighting in all the various kinds of aquatic-themed art.

My friend is dead, she kept telling herself silently. *I saw her murdered body.* But she couldn't quite believe it. The entire journey seemed surreal, which was perhaps appropriate given where she was—another opulent palace under the sea—to say nothing of the method of travel itself. But any joy had been wrung from the wonder of it all. Beneath the shiny veneer of this marvel, a palpable

madness lurked; it was very real and very deadly. Rosalind
half expected to wake at any moment, to find herself back
in London, Cecily and Charles with her.

Wandering back toward the train, she glanced at her
reflection in the polished glass of one of the windows. She
looked tired, drawn. A moment later, she caught a glimpse
of a figure behind her. As she continued on her way, she
managed to get a look at him out of the corner of her
eye and saw Bauer's agent—the same one from yesterday,
the one masquerading as the librarian—following her at
a distance.

It wasn't all that subtle, and perhaps that was the point.
It was a reminder that this was no dream. This was real,
and it was in her best interest to keep her thoughts silent.

As she stepped away from the train, she was startled to
spot Alix and Jacob emerging from one of the First Class
cars, arm in arm. They were going for a stroll as well, it
seemed. Alix wore a conservative dress colored dark blue
and together they looked rather somber. But they seemed
unusually . . . well, *close.* Had Alix spent time with him last
night, after she'd left Rosalind?

Catching sight of her, Jacob raised his hand in greeting.
Alix waved excitedly. Rosalind crossed the concourse and
met them halfway, below a mural of a seahorse.

"Good morning, Fräulein Wallace," Jacob said, giving
a stiff bow. "I do hope you are well." He lowered his voice.
"Under the circumstances."

So Jacob knew as well, did he? Rosalind wondered
who had told him. Had it been Erich? Or had it been
Alix? Or had he known all along? Perhaps it didn't even

matter. The train was small, and everyone was bound to find out sooner or later.

"A very pleasant morning to you as well, Lieutenant," she said, extending her hand with the warmest smile she could muster.

Before Rosalind knew what was happening, Alix had swept her up in a tight hug. "Oh, um . . ." she stammered, extricating herself. "And good morning to you, Alix. Are you well?"

"I am . . ." Alix paused, searching for the right words. Finally she shrugged. "I am very well, thank you. I have been doing some thinking. It is very good for me."

"Thinking is very good for a person," Rosalind agreed cautiously. "And what have you been thinking about?"

"I cannot say," Alix answered, sounding pleased. "It is a surprise."

Rosalind blinked a few times. "Oh," she said. "Well, I shan't pry."

But she very much wanted to, as Alix seemed to have completely forgotten about Cecily's death, or about her grief over it. Rosalind wondered for an instant if the girl had gone mad. But no, Jacob would have noticed. Perhaps he would have even sought Rosalind's counsel.

"I must confess, I am surprised to see anyone out this early," Rosalind said in the silence.

Jacob chuckled. "Oh, a man cannot be in the army and also be a late riser. It simply isn't done. I never sleep past breakfast."

She smiled a little. He was so boisterous and enthusiastic, almost like a little child. And while she would never utter the thought out loud, he struck her as not terribly bright; but that only added to his childlike charm and sincerity. It was difficult not to feel cheerful around him. Perhaps that was why Alix had sought his company.

"Good morning, everyone," a voice called.

Rosalind turned to see Erich approaching, looking very smart in a cream-colored suit. His expression was appropriately solemn. He nodded to each of them in turn. "Jacob, my friend; Lady von Hessen; and of course, Fräulein Wallace."

So at least he had the decorum not to speak informally to her in public. Rosalind had worried about that a little since their time together in the arboretum, about her confession. But it seemed Erich truly was a gentleman. He did not intend to take liberties of any sort.

"Good morning, Herr Steiner," Rosalind said.

She extended her hand to him. Erich took it gently and bowed to her, all the while holding her eyes. Rosalind felt a tingle at his touch, followed almost instantly by a wrenching emptiness deep inside her. Cecily should be at the receiving end of that gaze, her hand in his. Rosalind quickly withdrew and looked away.

"I'm surprised to see you awake this early, Herr Steiner," Alix said. "I thought that you would still be abed, like all proper gentlemen."

Erich tried his best to be cheerful. "Nonsense. If it is a gentleman you want, you should look to my dear friend Jacob. He is the one with the proper breeding. I am but the son of a humble businessman."

Jacob snorted. "'Humble,' he says! I know the old Herr

Steiner well. He is many things, God bless him, but humble is not one."

"That is true, God knows," Erich agreed easily. "But still, I am just a man of the people. Of humble origin."

"And a lot of money," Rosalind noted, doing her best to keep the mood light.

"The two go together very well," Erich replied in a dry voice. He held her gaze again. This time, she did not look away.

Alix cleared her throat. "The lieutenant and I had plans to take a stroll around the station before they seat us for lunch."

"I am looking forward to lunch," Jacob said happily.

"Aren't you always?" Erich noted with a good-natured nudge.

"Would Herr Steiner and Fräulein Wallace care to join us?" Alix asked. "A stroll is just the thing for an appetite."

"I agree," Rosalind said.

As she turned back to Erich, she had the distinct feeling she was falling, as if the world had become an abyss with no bottom; she had no idea what would become of her, of any of them, or if she should even bother to care . . . at least beyond what was happening right now, in this moment.

"Then it is settled." Erich held out his arm to Rosalind. "Shall we?"

○ ○ ○

It wasn't until much later that Rosalind felt herself snap out of whatever trance she had succumbed to over the course of the day. Quite suddenly, dressed in a ball gown, standing in the grand concourse, she felt jolted awake. She'd had a wonderful day, a wonderful dinner; but how was that possible? Her best friend was dead. As she waited for the arrival of her new friends—acquaintances, really; people she barely knew—she watched the line of Second Class passengers as they were herded up into the gallery. At Neptune Station, they were tossed a proverbial bone; they could *watch* the ball, but of course they couldn't participate. Dancing was a First Class privilege only. But, oh, how lucky they were to be let out to watch . . . or so Father's thinking went.

Rosalind began to shiver, even though the temperature was perfect. She felt sick and angry. And she couldn't tell whether she was upset because of the parade of the "lesser" passengers—all of whom looked quite happy to be let out, if only to watch the First Class passengers dance—or because of Cecily's conspicuous absence. Rosalind's friend had lived for balls like this.

Perhaps a bit of both, she thought. But no; it was more. She thought of Inspector Bauer, of how dismissive and contemptuous he was of those in Second Class, of how certain he was that Cecily's murderer had to be one of *them*. One of those lesser humans.

"I thought I might find you hiding somewhere," a voice said in her ear. "Your gown is a wonder."

Rosalind turned away, trying not to take any pleasure in how dashing Erich looked himself. She didn't want to disappoint him, but she was in no mood for dancing. "I am not hiding," she replied. "I am contemplating."

"Are they not much the same thing?" Erich asked, perhaps trying to evoke some laughter. "What is troubling you, Rosalind? Cecily?"

"Of course," Rosalind answered. "I keep thinking that I've accepted this. That she is gone, that the . . . the shock cannot get any worse. And then I think about her, lying there, dead, and it does get worse. One minute, I'm well; the next, I'm a wreck. And then . . ." She stopped. *The idea! Speaking to this boy so openly. What must he think of me?* "I apologize. This is none of your concern. I shouldn't be troubling you with all of this—"

"No," Erich said. "No, no. You need to talk about this. If it will help, I should like to be the one to listen."

Rosalind gave a slow nod.

"I am grateful for that . . . Erich," she said.

Erich reached out and touched her cheek. Rosalind tensed, but his fingers were warm and soft and she did not pull away. But then she remembered herself and quickly turned, lest someone see them.

"As I told you before," he said, "I am so very sorry for the death of your friend. If there were any way I could have prevented it, *for you*, I would gladly have done so."

"The . . . sentiment is appreciated," Rosalind said, still half turned away. "But I fear that there was nothing any of us could have done."

"Yes," Erich agreed. "Who can fathom the criminal mind? What drives a man to steal? To kill?"

Rosalind looked at him again, suddenly torn between trusting him and trusting no one. She glanced around. There was no sign of Inspector Bauer's men in the vicinity.

Had they given her the night off? Or had they simply lost track of her? More likely they were hidden from view, but watching all the while.

"Erich," she murmured before she could think better of it, "I am going to tell you something that I probably shouldn't tell you. It may very well put us both in danger."

Erich drew closer. "Yes? What is it? Please, you can tell me anything."

"I don't believe that Cecily was killed for her jewels," Rosalind whispered. "In fact, I'm certain that is not what happened." She fought to collect her thoughts. "I don't believe it was about robbery. I know it sounds strange, but I remember seeing her jewelry laid out on the table. None of it had been touched. And I know you'll say a man might panic after killing two people. But to have the courage to commit murder and then not to take the very jewels for which he'd murdered? I cannot believe that."

Erich frowned. "I see," he said slowly.

"As do I," Rosalind insisted. "I *saw*. I remember everything about that room. Like it is a picture in front of me. Every time I close my eyes, I see . . ." She shook herself. "That's not important. What matters is that there is something else going on. I don't know if Inspector Bauer and the others have the right man, but even if they do, I am certain his motive was not the one they suspect."

Erich ran his fingertips along his chin. Rosalind wondered if she had offended him with her talk about the murder. But after a little while, he turned back to her, his lips pressed into a tight line.

"You know," he said, "I think that may be so. But until

you spoke of Bauer and the wrong man in custody, I had been trying to dispel this terrible thought of mine."

"You agree with me?" Rosalind gasped.

Erich's face grew grim. The light that had always been there seemed to have been extinguished from his eyes. "Yes, and it is worse than that. I think . . . I fear . . . that my friend may have had something to do with it."

"Your friend? You mean Jacob?" Rosalind stared at him. "What on earth for? That's impossible—"

"One would think, yes?" he interrupted, avoiding her eyes. "But I think . . . I think Cecily may have been killed by Jacob and Alix together."

Rosalind was speechless. "But why?" she demanded.

"That I do not know," Erich replied. "But I have given it some thought. The two of them seem a little too familiar for people who have only just met. Surely you have noticed that?"

He nodded toward the dance floor. Indeed, as if he'd magically conjured the display for proof, there were Alix and Jacob, spinning through the crowd, entwined, almost rapturous.

"I . . . Well, I just assumed Alix was coping with the death of our friend by trying to forget it," Rosalind stammered, unable to stop gaping at them. "And Jacob was a distraction . . ." She turned back to Erich. "Forgive me for what I'm about to say. I know he's your friend, but he's not terribly intelligent. I don't think he could do it."

Erich averted his eyes once more. He appeared visibly ashamed to be harboring such evil thoughts. "I used to think as you do of him. That he was a happy-go-lucky sort, a committed soldier, a personable companion, nothing more. But I've never spent time with him like this, in such close quarters. There are certain things that Jacob has said since we arrived . . . certain things I have seen him do when he thought I was not watching."

Rosalind felt her heart thudding in her chest. "What has he done?"

Erich sighed. He forced a smile at her. "No. I cannot do this. I cannot betray his confidences. I must beg your pardon. I should not talk about Jacob like this. It could all be coincidence. Here I am, impugning my friend's reputation on conjecture, without a piece of evidence."

Rosalind nodded, as much out of frustration as out of admiration for this boy she'd only just met. She could hardly expect him to tell her the sordid details of his friend's conduct when there might be no actual connection to the murder; it was incredible enough that Erich had told her of his suspicions in the first place—and that he even had them.

"I won't pry," she assured him, "but I won't assume that Alix *or* Jacob were involved without proof."

"Thank you," Erich said, sounding relieved. "I suppose I shouldn't have said anything. It is only that . . . I want to help you, Rosalind. And I promise you this: whoever is behind the death of your dear friend—Jacob, Alix, even the captain of the train—I will not rest until I find the culprit. I will not rest until you have justice."

Rosalind laid a hand on his arm. She was troubled by his words, his tone, his outlandish theory that Alix von Hessen was a murderer. But at the same time, she believed in his intention: he did want to help her. And he had his own reasons, clearly, if he thought his friend was not a friend at all, but rather a criminal in disguise . . . "To have justice, we will need evidence," she said. "Something we can bring to the police."

"Agreed," Erich said. "We will begin with Jacob and Lady von Hessen. God willing, we may eliminate them as suspects."

"A faint heart never solved a mystery," Rosalind said, as much to herself as to him. Secretly, she prayed that they *could* be eliminated. Again she felt that terrible weight of memory. Her two best friends, her hosts for a joyous and carefree spring, were *gone*. One dead, one missing. Her heart thudded again. Perhaps Charles had been murdered, too, before they'd boarded the train? Or perhaps he'd sensed mortal danger and had run to protect himself? But no, Cecily would have been panicked in either instance . . .

"We will watch them," Erich continued. "Like hawks, yes? You will watch your friend Lady von Hessen. I will watch my friend Jacob. If she reveals anything, you come to me. If he reveals anything, I come to you. And together we will go to Inspector Bauer and force him to see the truth."

"Do you think it will work?" Rosalind asked, snapping back into the present, forcing herself to focus on some course of action over which she could have a semblance of control. She peered out at the dance floor, where Alix and Jacob were still twirling.

"It is the only thing we can do. So we must hope that it works."

"And if it isn't them?" she asked.

Erich sighed. "Then we will have a very long list of suspects."

She drew closer, narrowing the distance between them. "Why are you doing this for me?" she asked. "You didn't even know my friend."

"As I said, I had my own suspicions," Erich replied. "You simply brought them to light. And besides, though I may not be a dashing officer, a man does like to think that he may be a hero to a beautiful young woman from time to time."

Rosalind couldn't help but smile at the compliment, though she felt awkward doing it. "You make a very good knight-errant," she said. "All you need is the shining armor."

Erich extended his hand. "That I cannot obtain. But I wonder, Fräulein Wallace, if you would be so very kind as to join me in the next dance."

Rosalind hesitated. She wanted to ever so much, but she found herself unable to put Cecily out of her mind. Everything had happened so quickly, so unexpectedly, so awfully. Then again, it *was* a ball. And a dance was only a dance. Cecily would have danced. Moreover, she would have wanted *Rosalind* to dance, so that she could pretend to be scandalized. Rosalind could almost hear her old friend's carefree giggle.

"Herr Steiner," Rosalind said. She took his hand, smiling and fighting back tears at the same time. "I thought you might never ask."

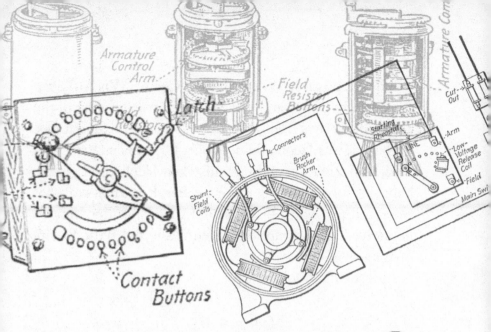

Upon the train's departure from Neptune Station the next morning, Rosalind met Alix in her room. And as instructed, she spent the next few hours watching the girl "like a hawk." Not that she particularly minded; nor was it particularly difficult to watch her. They'd adjourned to the Red Parlor after breakfast and sat together until lunch. Whatever had sparked Alix's bizarre fervor the other night, the flame had died. Now Alix was simply sad, appropriately so. She spent the entire morning talking of Cecily, of the adventures they'd shared at school, of Cecily's troublemaking and generosity and joie de vivre. She and Rosalind had both wept as often as they'd laughed.

By midafternoon Rosalind was certain Erich's suspicions were entirely unfounded. What reason could Alix possibly have for killing Cecily? Was Alix even capable of killing someone? She was a true product of the aristocracy, sheltered and naive about so many things. Perhaps it was Jacob's doing alone. Or perhaps Erich had a wild imagination and had mistaken Jacob's odd private behavior for something more sinister. Regardless of what the truth proved to be, Rosalind was determined not to be swayed by assumptions, even if she did trust Erich's own motives.

And she did. Didn't she?

○ ○ ○

Rosalind finally parted company with Alix in the late evening. As she made her way down the corridor back to her own compartment, she realized she was not the least bit tired. She didn't wish to go to the library and engage with that phony librarian, but she needed something to help her fall asleep. Perhaps listening to a little music on the gramophone by her bedside would do the trick. Otherwise she might be reduced to pacing back and forth.

When she entered her room, she felt certain that something was out of place. At first she did not know what. Her things were as she had left them, strewn about, and a quick check showed that she was alone. She turned in circles until she spotted what was different: a cylinder lay in the receiving tray of the pneumatic post machine.

How odd.

Who could possibly be sending her messages? Not

Alix, surely; they had only just parted. Erich, perhaps? She smiled a little at the thought. Then her smile faded. More likely Inspector Bauer, inquiring about whether she was satisfied with the performance of his spies . . .

Rosalind opened the cylinder and unfolded the slip of paper within. It was a short note, only three lines long, but it was enough to make her dizzy:

I am alive. I am on the train.
Meet me in the last baggage car at midnight.
I will explain everything.

At first she thought it might be from Cecily—impossible though that was—but there could be no mistaking the handwriting.

It belonged to Charles.

Rosalind dropped the cylinder and sank to the floor, her head swimming. Charles? On the train all this time? But how was that possible? Why hadn't he boarded with them? Why hadn't he said something before now? Why hadn't he been there when Cecily was killed?

Rosalind shut her eyes tightly and concentrated on breathing for a short while. It was all just a dream, she thought. Some insane fever dream. She was at home, deathly ill. Cecily was still alive. None of this was real.

But when her lids fluttered open, she was still clutching the note. Cecily was dead, and her brother was alive, demanding to meet in the last baggage car at midnight. Rosalind's chest felt tight, as if she couldn't suck enough air into her lungs. She forced herself to stand. She needed to get out, away from the blasted train and its claustrophobic compartments. She needed to think.

Stumbling to the door, she braced herself against it and straightened. She couldn't lurch through the hallways like a madwoman. No, she needed to compose herself. Nobody could see that her heart was pounding. Nobody could see the panic inside, provided she kept an even keel. After another deep breath, she opened the door and went outside. There was no one in the corridor, which was good. Most of the cars were deserted, in fact. As she made her way toward the rear of the train, she passed only an occasional porter. It was a little past ten o'clock, and it appeared most of the passengers had gone to bed.

When she reached the arboreal car, she managed something approximating a relaxed state. She wandered up and down the paths for a few minutes, collecting her thoughts. Once or twice she stood still and closed her eyes, listening to the birdsong.

I didn't know there were birds here, she thought.

Ah, but of course, they weren't real. Just a recording played on the speakers to help with the ambience. What *was* real aboard this train? It was so hard to distinguish . . .

"Good evening, Rosalind," said a voice from behind her. "Fancy meeting you here."

Rosalind's eyes popped open, and she whirled around in surprise. For a moment it felt like her heart had stopped. But there was no cause for concern. Quite the contrary: it was Erich. He stood a few paces away, smiling at her, still in his evening finery.

"I am sorry, I did not mean to startle you," he apologized.

Rosalind shook her head. "It's fine. I have simply been . . . confounded this evening."

Erich tilted his head and approached her. "You are upset," he said.

"It's nothing to worry about," Rosalind assured him.

"But it is everything to worry about," Erich replied. "I do not want you to be upset, Rosalind. You are too wonderful to be upset."

Rosalind laughed in spite of herself, and it made her feel quite foolish. She drew in a breath. "It has simply been a very trying day. And yet it hasn't at all. And that is what's so peculiar. I watched Alix, as we agreed I'd do . . . and I saw nothing untoward or suspicious. We both mourned."

"Your friend's death is weighing on you," Erich said with a nod. "I understand that."

"Yes," Rosalind said. "And it has just become fresh for me again."

Erich took her hand and gently raised it to his lips. "I want you to know that I am here for you, Rosalind," he whispered. "I want to comfort you. I would do anything in my power to make your sadness go away."

"Erich—"

"You are such a beautiful woman," Erich continued, his eyes aflame. "I simply cannot put into words how marvelous you are . . . ." And then he pulled her into his arms and kissed her. It was wonderful, and delicious, and Rosalind felt herself being swept away, dizzy and delighted and confused, until she could think of nothing but the kiss. The kiss and . . .

Charles.

Rosalind gasped and pulled away. She held on to Erich's coat for a moment as she tried to steady herself. Breathing heavily, she looked up and managed to say, "Wait. I'm sorry. Wait."

Erich straightened. His lips quivered as he fought not to appear hurt.

"Have I done something wrong?" he asked. "I am sorry, but I thought . . . I have great affection for you. I thought that you felt the same."

"I do," Rosalind said. But no, that wasn't quite true, and she couldn't lie about such a thing, even to soothe his feelings. "I don't."

"I am confused," Erich said. "You say one thing, then another. What am I to think?"

Rosalind shook her head. "Erich, you are a wonderful man. I thank you so much for your kindness, but there is someone else."

A long and uncomfortable pause fell between them.

"Ah," Erich finally said with a sad smile. Yet he seemed relieved that a rival suitor was the cause of the rejection, not any fault of his own. "I am sorry, I did not know."

"How could you have known?" Rosalind said. "I would have spoken sooner, but I didn't realize . . ."

"Yes, of course," Erich said, looking away. He was silent for a time. But presently he looked back at Rosalind and forced a disappointed smile. "I hope you will forgive me for having been so forward."

"All is forgiven, absolutely," Rosalind promised him. "I'm flattered, Erich, truly I am. But my heart belongs to another, and you deserve better than to be deceived about such a thing."

Erich gave a thoughtful nod. "I appreciate that, yes," he said. After a moment, he asked, "Will you tell me who it is? Someone else on the train?" He chuckled, sounding very sad. "I hope it is not Jacob. He always steals the girls, you know. And I am still not certain he's innocent . . ."

Rosalind took Erich's hands and squeezed them. She wanted to be comforting and reassuring, but she had no idea how to do that without giving him the wrong impression all over again.

Erich managed a smile. "Whoever this man of yours is, he is very fortunate."

"It's . . ." Rosalind began, hesitating. "It's Cecily's brother, Charles." So strange: until she'd said the words out loud, she hadn't fully admitted the truth to herself.

"Ahhhh," Erich said. "Ah, yes, it becomes more clear. Then he is indeed fortunate, in spite of the tragedy that has befallen his family. At least he is not on the train. I daresay if he were to learn about my courting you, he would find me and punch me in the nose. And my nose is very dear to me. It is one of my best features. All the girls say so."

Rosalind tried her best to laugh for his benefit. But Erich's attempt to deflect his embarrassment and rejection with humor made Rosalind feel all the worse. The kiss had betrayed where both their feelings lay. Still, he deserved to know the truth, insofar as she knew it herself.

"That's the funny thing," she said. "I . . . I think he may actually be on the train with us. Not that I would tell him about this," she quickly added. "Simply a misunderstanding. It will stay between us, I promise you."

"He's on the train?" Erich asked in disbelief. "But that is impossible. He left you at Hamburg, did he not?"

"He did," Rosalind said. "Simply vanished." Her eyes narrowed. "But how did you know that?"

"You mentioned it, of course," Erich replied. "Perhaps it was Cecily. I'm certain it came up in conversation. But you say he is on the train?"

Rosalind frowned, her mind whirling. "Erich, may I confide in you a second time? Even after this?"

"I hope that I am still your friend, Rosalind. Of course, you may tell me anything."

Rosalind drew the crumpled note from her sleeve and showed it to Erich. "It's Charles's handwriting," she said.

Erich's eyes widened as they roved over the words. "Are you certain?" he asked. He sounded very worried. "It is unsigned, and this person asks you to go to one of the baggage cars in the middle of the night? I do not trust this, Rosalind. Truly, I do not."

"You don't want me to go, do you?"

He sighed. "You are going to go regardless, aren't you?"

"Yes," Rosalind said. "I understand that there is a risk and I appreciate your concern. But I *know* that handwriting. Signed or not, it is Charles. And I need to know what is going on—"

"This is a very bad idea, Rosalind," he interrupted. "A very bad one."

"You can't stop me," she warned, seeing where he was going.

"No, no, I would never do such a thing," Erich said quickly. "But, um, perhaps you might allow me to accompany you. I would not stay . . . I'll tell you what: meet me here at one quarter to midnight. We will go together. I will escort you through Second Class and the staff quarters, and if it truly is your Charles, I will leave the two of you alone. But if it is some sort of trap by persons nefarious, I would rather be there than to learn of it afterward."

Rosalind bit her lip. She felt a twinge of guilt for how he must feel. But she could not change her heart any more than he could change his. "If you insist," she said. "It is very kind of you. I . . ." She broke off at the sound of rustling in the leaves of one of the nearby trees. She turned to look but could see nothing in the shadows. Was someone watching them?

"Did you hear something?" she asked.

Erich listened for a moment and shook his head.

"No," he answered. "Did you?"

Rosalind swallowed. "No matter. But I think we should part ways now, to be safe."

Erich nodded and whispered back, "I will meet you right here at a quarter to midnight, yes?"

"Agreed," Rosalind said. "And . . . thank you, Erich."

He gave her one last melancholy smile. "For you, anything."

○   ○   ○

Back in her room, Rosalind regretted departing from
Erich. Alone, time turned to molasses as she alternately
paced and stared at the clock in the hopes that it might be
made to move faster. She changed out of her gown into
the simplest dress she owned—it allowed for running,
if necessary. She even entertained the thought of going
to the rendezvous early, but there was no guarantee that
Charles would even be there before midnight. Indeed,
there was no guarantee that Charles would be there at all.
Erich was right to worry.

When the clock finally showed eleven forty, Rosalind walked as swiftly as she could to the arboreal car,
self-conscious in her futile effort to maintain something resembling poise. She followed the main path to
their appointed meeting point—the spot where she'd
left Erich only an hour and a half earlier—and stopped
abruptly.

There was no sign of him.

Rosalind turned in a slow circle, peering into every
shrub and tree and flower bed. She held her breath, listening for a telltale rustle of leaves, quiet footsteps on the
flagstones. Nothing. She turned back to the door from
whence she'd come, expecting him to appear. He simply
wasn't here.

Had Erich changed his mind and decided to abandon
her? Not that she would be surprised, given how she'd
spurned his advances. Nor would it change her mind
about the rendezvous. She fully intended to find Charles,

with or without Erich's help. But it seemed unlike Erich to have broken his word.

Rosalind stepped toward the rear of the car. A shadow under a nearby clump of bright azaleas caught her eye—and she froze. It wasn't a shadow; it was a body.

Her knees turned to jelly as she knelt down, her legs nearly collapsing under her. In an instant she knew why Erich had not arrived: he was already here.

Here . . . but gone. Dead. Of that she had no doubt.

As Rosalind pushed aside the rough and brittle branches, her breath started coming fast. Her eyes roved over his suit, stained with the arboretum's soil. His eyes were closed, his face as white as ivory, a stark contrast to the blood pooled and caked around his upper body. He must have been stabbed somewhere . . . Whoever had killed him had tried to conceal the corpse but hadn't done a thorough job. Perhaps the murderer had been in a rush.

Rosalind began to tremble uncontrollably. She forced herself to stand, clinging to the brush for support. Her head swam. Poor Erich! This boy was dead because of her. Her eyes fell once more to the bloody corpse, and her body seized. At that moment, she spotted the murder weapon. It was still lodged in his neck. It was so slender that she hadn't seen it at first. But there was no mistaking what it was: a hatpin.

A hatpin shaped like a peacock feather.

Oh my God, Rosalind thought, recoiling more from the revelation than from the horror beside her. *Erich was right all along.*

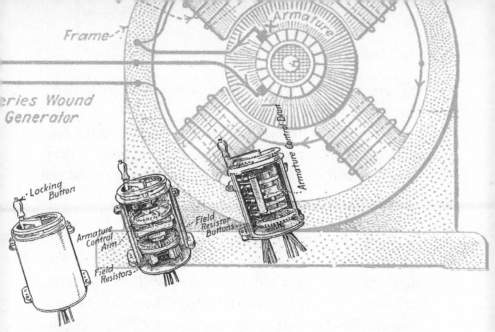

However much it pained Rosalind to leave Erich's body in the bushes, she had no choice. It was almost midnight. Charles or no Charles, she would do as the note had bidden. The note represented her last hope, her only chance to find an explanation for this nightmare.

Either that or she could return to her room, perhaps to be murdered by Alix as well. Or she could report the body to train security, thereby allowing Inspector Bauer to take control both of the investigation and of her very life for the remainder of the journey. He was already hostile toward her. She knew how Father's trains operated, too: she would be placed under arrest—"for her safety" or some similar nonsense—locked away with no hope of ever learning the truth.

On the other hand, she would be safe.

Or would she? If Bauer and his men had been

any good at their jobs, three passengers would still be alive.

Turning away from Erich, she made for Second Class, forcing herself not to look back or second-guess the decision. She had a purpose and she would not be swayed from it.

As she hurried through the last cars of the train, Rosalind was struck by the contrast to First Class, a contrast that only grew more pronounced the farther she went. Second Class was still comfortable, still clean. The metal was polished; the windows were washed. But the carpeting was coarser. The corridors were more cramped, the compartments more tightly packed. There were half as many carriages for an equal number of passengers.

And once Rosalind entered the crew cars, all pretense had been abandoned. They were sparse and functional, and clearly not for public viewing. For people like Doris, for people like those silent porters and the waiter who'd brought her breakfast. *The Serving Class*, she thought. The invisible. Here, at this late hour, some were out and about, joking and drinking ale in the cramped halls. Rosalind caught a few curious stares, but she kept her head down and plowed forward.

When she finally reached the baggage cars, she heard some raised voices and the beginnings of a commotion behind her. No doubt Erich's body had been found; now the staff was being roused to help secure the train. Well, good. At least maybe they'd be able to apprehend Alix. Rosalind reminded herself to remain in the moment, not to care about what came next. All that mattered was finding Charles.

The guard on duty at the baggage car door had fallen asleep. He was a portly fellow, with his head tilted back and his mouth open, snoring loudly. A mug of coffee sat almost full on the floor beside his chair. Tiptoeing around him and holding her breath, Rosalind tried the door. It was unlocked. Her pulse quickened as she stepped inside and gently shut the door behind her.

Thankfully the baggage cars were lit with the same electric lamps as the rest of the train, but here they were bare, lacking any sort of glass covering to soften them. She squinted in the harsh glare as she dashed past racks of luggage and stacks of crates lashed to the floor with leather straps to keep them from sliding.

She placed her hand on the door to the last car and took a deep breath.

When she stepped inside, she exhaled.

The carriage was empty.

Rosalind very nearly swore aloud. She was tired, and frightened, and at the end of her wits. Was Charles dead, too? Was *everyone* dead? Jacob as well? Had Alix murdered everyone Rosalind had met since boarding the train in Hamburg?

As if in answer to her silent questions, a pair of strong arms seized her from behind. She tried to scream for help. A hand clamped down on her mouth, muting the sound. Her eyes bulged. She struggled to twist away. In the reflection of a darkened window she caught a glimpse of a porter's uniform.

So it *had* been a trap. Erich had been right. But of course, that was why he was dead. Being right was a rather hollow victory for the dead. *That will not be me*, Rosalind thought, panic turning to fury.

She would *not* be murdered by some strange conspirator in a baggage car on her father's train.

Kicking backward violently, Rosalind drove the heel of her boot against her attacker's shin. He cried out in pain. His grip loosened just enough for her to wriggle free. She spun around, and nearly shrieked.

"Charles! What in God's name are you doing?"

He hobbled backward, leaning down to rub his shin.

"Being kicked by you, Rose," he groaned. "I see my message reached you. I suppose I should have signed it, but I couldn't trust that Bauer wouldn't be reading the mail."

"How did you do it?" Rosalind asked. "Send the message?"

Charles smiled slightly. "A porter can go almost anywhere without being noticed. I simply waited until everyone was preoccupied with dinner and then I sent the message from the machine in the stewards' carriage. I could have broken into someone's room to do it, but that would have been rude."

"Very rude," Rosalind agreed dryly. *As rude as abandoning someone in Hamburg.*

Charles grinned at her, but a moment later he slumped down on one of the boxes and winced, rubbing his injured leg again. "You're quite strong, you know."

"You shouldn't sneak up on a girl," Rosalind said.

"I realize that now," Charles grumbled. "I assumed it was you, but right now I can't be too careful. And I wanted to be sure you weren't followed—"

"What are you doing here?" Rosalind demanded.

"Rosalind, please let me explain," he began. He stopped rubbing his shin and leaned forward. "There are—"

"Cecily's dead, Charles," she barked at him, cutting him off again. She thought that seeing him might make her swoon, but the opposite was true: she was enraged, unable to keep her voice from shaking. "Did you know?"

Charles inhaled deeply and looked down. He nodded.

"I did . . . I do," he said. "But . . . to my shame . . . I learned she was in danger too late. I thought that disappearing in Hamburg would give the two of you some distance from me. I was wrong."

"What are you talking about?"

Charles rose to his feet, limping a little. After a moment, he steadied himself, a little gingerly, on his injured leg. He looked into Rosalind's eyes with an expression of the utmost seriousness and said simply, "I'm a spy."

Rosalind laughed. She couldn't help herself. "What?"

"I am serious."

"A spy. Since when?"

"Since I was sixteen," Charles answered. "Not very long, really," he admitted, "but I've been training most of my life, in the de Vere tradition."

"Charles." Rosalind pronounced his name slowly. "You're not making any sense. You realize that, don't you?"

"I assure you, it is true," Charles replied. "My family, the de Veres, have served the English Crown for scores of generations. *Scores.* Since the reign of King John, we have worked to preserve England from all threats, within and without. Even now, my father advises King Edward on matters of intelligence."

"All right, now I *do* understand what I am hearing," Rosalind told him, "and I am quite certain you've lost your mind."

"That is a shame, Rosalind, because it is true," Charles said. "And unfortunately, against our best intentions, it seems you have been dragged into it."

Rosalind folded her arms. "I am well aware that I've been dragged into *something*, Charles. Something that cost your sister her life. So yes. Please. Explain."

"Cecily should never have come," Charles muttered, shaking his head. "But she and I assumed that if we traveled with you—you, the daughter of the railway's owner—we would be above suspicion. And of course, there was also the hope that being so young, we might be overlooked where an older agent would be found out. That was always the problem, you see: getting someone onboard to carry out the work. But then your father wanted you to take the inaugural voyage. It was too perfect a chance to miss."

"A chance? What chance?" Rosalind asked, growing angrier by the second. "What are you talking about?" It was not just Charles's implication that she was simply a pawn in some scheme that upset her. Worse than that was the very notion that Cecily of all people had used their friendship for some other purpose. But could she even believe that? It was too far-fetched. Cecily was so flighty, so devilish, so clueless: hardly the sort of person who could be involved in any sort of plot . . .

Unless she wasn't flighty at all. And in that moment, Rosalind felt everything she had taken for granted crumbling into pieces around her. Nothing was what it seemed. Worse: anything, no matter how horrid, was possible. Perhaps Charles really was a spy. Perhaps she *was* nothing more than a pawn.

Charles held out his hands in an effort to calm her. "Rosalind, please," he said. "We weren't using you, not really. It was just that the coincidences were too perfect—"

"What are you doing on the train, Charles? Just tell me."

He took a deep breath.

"We're going to blow up the tunnel."

Rosalind stared at him, once again silenced by the horrible and abject absurdity of what had popped out of his mouth.

"Why?" she eventually managed. "Why would you want to blow up the train? There are people on it. Innocent people."

"Not the train," Charles corrected. "The tunnel."

"What's the difference?"

"The difference is that no one is going to be hurt," Charles answered. "It's very simple. We have a bomb—"

"*A bomb?*"

"It's set on a timer. As we approach the shores of America, I will arm it and decouple the baggage car. By the time the bomb blows up, the train will be safely on land. No harm done, but some lost luggage."

How could Charles speak so blithely about this?

Furious, Rosalind rushed forward and struck him in the chest with her fists.

"You're mad!" she shouted. "Mad!"

Charles grabbed her hands to stop her, as gently as he could.

"I'm not mad," he grunted as she squirmed. "It has to be done. And don't you think that if Bauer was willing to murder Cecily, there's a damn good reason for our wanting to do it?"

Rosalind finally wrenched herself away and backed off. Her lungs were heaving. "Bauer?" she gasped. "He killed Cecily?"

"Perhaps not himself, but he must have ordered it," Charles said. "He's an agent of the Prussian Secret Police. They sent him and his men to protect the tunnel from us. One of them recognized me in Hamburg before we boarded . . ."

"The man with the mustache," Rosalind whispered.

He nodded. "That's why I had to disappear. But I hadn't realized they suspected Cecily as well. I'd never have allowed her to go if I'd known."

"You've got a right to feel guilty about that," Rosalind said, still seething. "They may have killed her, but it's your fault she's dead. And why would you want to blow up my father's tunnel?"

Charles took a few steps toward her, limping slightly. He tried to touch her shoulder, but Rosalind jerked away. "It's not about you or your family, Rose," he said. "It's about England and Germany. This tunnel . . . It's not only for passengers. It's meant to give Germany a lifeline to America in the event of a war with the British Empire."

He sat back on a crate and rested his hands on his knees. He winced again. She'd really hurt him.

Well, good. He deserved it, Rosalind thought.

"The facts speak for themselves," Charles said. "The tunnel is meant to safeguard the German supply line in the event of war against a superior naval power," Charles continued. "That means Britain. If war with Germany comes—and I'm certain it will—the Royal Navy will blockade them.

"But with this tunnel, Germany has a solution. They can run trainloads of supplies and munitions back and forth, month after month. We won't be able to stop them. Germany will be free to warmonger unchecked."

"My father would never agree to that," Rosalind protested.

Charles's face darkened. "It was your father's idea. How do you think he sold the Germans on the project?"

Rosalind looked away and thought it over. Was that possible? Could her father be conspiring with Germany? Not out of political allegiance, of course, but for money? Did he see war coming as well and plan to make yet another fortune supplying it? Of all the terrible secrets she'd uncovered about people she thought she knew, this one, sadly, was the least surprising.

Behind them, Rosalind heard the door to the carriage open. She and Charles both spun around. Charles drew a revolver from his pocket.

Rosalind gasped.

"Alix?"

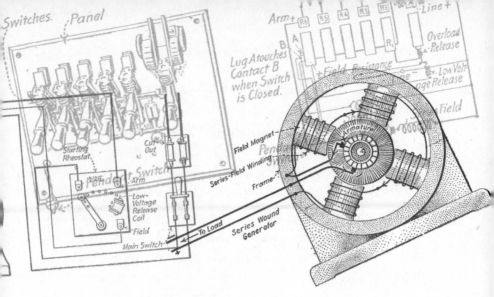

Rosalind found it increasingly hard to breathe. Alix quietly entered the carriage and closed the door behind her. In one hand the girl held a revolver, similar to the one Charles carried— not that Rosalind was any expert on pistols. She'd rarely seen one until this very night.

"Hello, Rosalind," Alix said, her voice calm and even. "I thought I would find you here." She smiled at Charles. "I overheard your friend here, ranting just now. You know, I find it a little tiring the way that the British go on and on about German empire building, as if we were the only people in Europe ever to have attempted such a thing. *Your* country controls a quarter of the globe and claims hundreds of millions of people as its subjects without asking their consent. Hypocritical, don't you think?"

Rosalind shook her head, suddenly very afraid.

Chapter Seventeen

She couldn't tear her eyes from Alix's pistol. The girl was clearly at ease with it.

"You're mad," she whispered. "You killed Erich."

"I did, yes," Alix admitted. "But Rosalind, you must understand, it's not what you think."

Charles turned to Rosalind. "Who is Erich?" he asked.

"A gentleman we met on the train," Rosalind said, her voice rising. "A very nice gentleman. And you murdered him. He was going to help me and you murdered him! With a *hat pin*—"

"Erich was not a gentleman, Rosalind," Alix said. "He was an enemy."

Charles narrowed his eyes at Alix. "Do I know you?"

She turned to him. "You don't recognize me? It has only been three years, Charles. I may have been just a slip of a girl at the time, but surely you recognize your sister's old school friend."

His jaw dropped. "Alix von Hessen!"

"As God made me." She gave Charles a polite curtsey, though never once turning her pistol away from him.

"You're a . . . German spy?" Charles whispered.

"I am *not* a German spy," Alix barked. "That is to say, I am German and I am a spy, but I am not a spy for Germany. I have far more important things to do than serve one petty empire or another."

Charles shook his head. He took a step toward her. "Rosalind is right. You *are* mad. Now why don't you put that gun down?"

Rosalind swallowed, thinking of the eagles at the Brandenburg station, thinking of how she and Cecily had joked about German pride. Alix had been the only one not laughing. Yet she was laughing now.

"Charles," Alix said after a deep breath, "I need Rosalind's father's marvel of a train to keep running. When war comes—and it will come, within twenty years, I expect—the British cannot be allowed to starve their enemies into submission."

Charles sniffed. "What would a spoiled little schoolgirl know about the winds of war?"

"I know many things," Alix said. "For example, I know that there is another tunnel. Below this one."

Rosalind blinked at her. "Of course there isn't . . ."

"Why? 'Of course there isn't,' because your father didn't tell you?" Alix mocked.

"I've seen all his plans and sketches. If there were a second tunnel—"

"You'd be the last to know," Alix finished. "You're his daughter. I almost didn't learn of it. But my sources are clearly better than yours, Englishman," she added, addressing Charles. "So you see, there is no point in your intended sabotage. It will slow the shipments, but it will not stop them."

Charles kept smiling, but Rosalind saw his jaw twitch. "You're bluffing."

Alix shrugged.

"Tell me something," he said. "Did you kill my sister? You did, didn't you? Like a viper slithering through the flower beds—"

"How very descriptive and also completely wrong," Alix snapped. "I did not kill Cecily. I would *never* have killed

Cecily. She was my dear friend." She looked at Rosalind. "Erich killed her, so I killed him."

Rosalind's insides turned to ice. Time seemed to freeze. Erich was Cecily's murderer? It couldn't be true. But if it was . . . She had trusted him, confided in him, told him of her suspicions, and all the while he had been the one?

"Impossible," Rosalind whispered.

"Is it?" Alix countered. "You're a bright girl, Rosalind. Think. He was an agent for Bauer. I suspect he either tried to interrogate her or was caught searching her compartment for information. In either case, he disposed of both Cecily and poor Doris. I am certain."

"You have proof?" Rosalind demanded.

"Of a kind. He knew too much about the official story, but he insisted on gossiping with us about the matter. I think he was trying to trick us into revealing what we knew, or what we suspected. I spent a whole day prodding Jacob for information about his friend. According to him, nobody gossiped at breakfast about the crime, as Erich reported. Jacob is quite the gossip himself; he would have remembered it. And that was when I knew. Erich was going to go with you to meet Charles and then kill you both." Alix smiled wickedly. "I warned him that if he was ungentlemanly toward you, I would kill him with a hatpin. He thought I was joking. I was not."

And suddenly it made sense.

"You were the one hiding in the bushes," Rosalind said.

Alix nodded.

Rosalind looked at her with growing understanding—a mutual understanding, it seemed.

"And who is Jacob?" Charles asked.

"Don't start being possessive of Rosalind, Charles," Alix teased. "You can't abandon a girl in a strange place and expect her to welcome you back with open arms."

Charles raised his revolver.

Rosalind held out her hands. "Could we perhaps put the guns away?" she said, fighting to keep her voice even.

"I will after she does," Charles said.

"And I will after he does," Alix mimicked.

Rosalind's shoulders sagged. "So much for being reasonable . . ."

"Being reasonable won't protect the British Empire," Charles declared, straightening.

"I am surprised an Englishman even knows the meaning of the word," Alix taunted. "Besides—"

The train shuddered. Rosalind felt her footing slip for a moment. Alix fell back against the closed door.

"Are we gaining speed?" Rosalind cried.

"We bloody well are," Charles confirmed.

The speakers in the carriage crackled to life: "Ladies and gentlemen, this is your captain speaking. Our most sincere apologies, but owing to some small problems of a purely technical nature, we will be accelerating to maximum speed and completing our journey well ahead of schedule. Unfortunately, this makes it impossible for us to stop at Columbia Station as planned. For your safety, please remain in your compartments. Remain seated whenever possible. We apologize for any inconvenience."

The train shook again.

Charles limped wildly, nearly losing his balance. But

at least he and Alix had shoved their guns in their belts, if only to remain standing. The sound of the locomotive and the clanking of the wheels grew louder. Rosalind half feared that they would derail.

"That wasn't part of the plan," Charles said, bracing himself against one of the shelves.

"What plan?" Alix asked. "To destroy the train?"

"Only the tunnel," Charles snapped. "Unlike you, I'm not a murderer."

"Quiet!" Rosalind shouted. "We have a problem. I think Bauer's men found Erich's body. That's why we're accelerating. They don't want the killer to have a chance to escape at the station."

"Smart girl," Alix said.

"Dammit." Charles limped over to a large leather case sitting alone on one of the bottom shelves at the back of the car.

"That's your bomb, isn't it?" Rosalind asked.

For a moment, Charles looked as if he might lie about it, but then he nodded. "Yes, it is, though it's not really *my* bomb."

"King Edward's bomb then, or Britannia's bomb, whatever you care to call it." Rosalind was in no mood to mince words.

"No, I mean it's Cecily's bomb," Charles explained. "Infiltration I can manage. Shooting I'm quite good at. Drugging a guard's coffee, I'm your man . . . But with bombs, I just set the dials the way they tell me to."

Rosalind was almost tempted to laugh again. "You don't really mean to say that *Cecily* built a bomb?"

"Of course," Charles said. "She's dashed good at it . . .
Was dashed good at it." He scowled. "She built the thing."

"I do not believe it," Alix agreed. "Cecily?"

"You didn't think she was really that foolish, did you?"
Charles said. "I mean, she was my sister after all."

At the doorway, Alix glanced through the window
and said, "Rosalind, you're right. We do have a problem.
Four armed men in the next carriage. And Bauer is one
of them."

Rosalind rushed to the door and peered into the next
car. She ducked away before Bauer was able to catch her
terrified stare. She recognized the other three men, too:
the man with the mustache, the sour man who'd posed
as the librarian, and the waiter who'd served her breakfast. All armed.

"That man with the mustache . . . Bauer told me that he
was in custody for Cecily's murder," she hissed.

"Of course he did, Rosalind," Alix said calmly. "It was
all a farce. They're all on the same side. Bauer wanted to
silence us, to hush the whole thing up. So he gave us a
guilty party. I suspect the man was going to conveniently
escape and go missing once we arrived in New York—
that is, assuming they even carried the pretense that far."

Rosalind tried not to panic. She turned back to Charles.

He was fiddling with the catches on the case. She
rushed across the room and grabbed for him.

"Don't you dare!" she shouted. "Don't you dare arm
that thing . . ."

Charles pulled away from her and snapped, "I'm not
going to arm it. I'm going to disarm it! Remove the

explosives! With how fast the train's moving, I can't trust when to release the baggage car. And I don't want anyone getting hurt. That was never part of the plan."

The train shook again and teetered sideways as it started to go around a wide curve. At a normal pace, the movement wouldn't have been noticeable, but at the train's current speed it swept them up with its force. Rosalind fell into Charles, Charles tumbled into some crates—and the luggage shelf broke free from its supports, tipped over, and crashed to the floor in a heap of wood and metal and baggage.

"Oh, bugger," Charles grunted.

He bounded to his feet, wincing in pain, but he hesitated long enough to help Rosalind stand. Alix struggled toward them. He tried in vain to reach the bomb, but it was buried at the very bottom of the pile. He strained and strained but he simply could not reach it. The train began to straighten and shimmy less. The car quieted.

Rosalind froze. She caught the faint but unmistakable sound of . . .

"Do you hear ticking?" she asked him.

Charles's face went white as a sheet. "Bugger, bugger, and bugger."

"It's the bomb, isn't it?" Rosalind asked, her throat dry, already knowing the answer. She began tugging at the pile harder than ever, though very little of it seemed to budge.

"It's been activated," Charles said. His voice shook.

Alix dashed back to the door. "You fool. Leave it to an Englishman to build a bomb he can't control—"

"*Cecily* built it," he growled. "But it's all clockwork." He and Rosalind struggled in vain to dislodge the debris. "When it hit the floor, the catch must have released and started the timer."

Rosalind grabbed Charles by his collar. "How long is the timer set for?" she asked.

"Thirty minutes . . ."

Thirty minutes?

Alix looked away from the window and called to them, "Bomb or no, I wager we have about another thirty seconds before Bauer and his men finish with their carriage and check this one." She looked again and gritted her teeth. "Forget it. Time's up. He's spotted us."

Rosalind spun around. "Alix, do something!" she cried. "Charles, help me move this damn shelf."

In horror, Rosalind stared as Alix pulled the door open a crack and fired two shots toward Bauer and the other men.

Rosalind had no idea if they hit their targets or not. Bauer started shouting in German, so she guessed not.

Charles moaned, struggling against the shelf, and the crates that pinned the bomb in place. "It's no use," he said, gasping for breath. "I can't move it. And if I can't move it, it's not moving until the bomb goes off."

"What are we going to do?" Alix called. "They ran for cover but I can't hold them off forever."

Rosalind just had to think. There had to be a solution. Something.

The speakers crackled to life once more. When the captain spoke this time, his voice betrayed unease, if not outright fear. "Ladies and gentlemen, this is your captain . . . We will shortly be passing through Columbia Station, though we will not be stopping. We encourage you to look out your windows and admire the view as it passes by. Again, we apologize for any inconvenience."

Rosalind narrowed her eyes. A germ of an idea began to form in her head. "New plan," she announced. "We decouple the baggage car at Columbia Station, hit the manual break, and escape on a submersible. All in favor?"

Charles blinked at her. He shot another glance at the bomb.

"That's . . . not half bad, as horrible ideas go—"

"I like it," Alix interrupted. She leaned against the door with her pistol raised, breathing heavily. "It is a good plan. In it, we do not die."

"I have always regarded that as one measure of a good plan, yes," Rosalind muttered.

"How do we do this?" Charles asked. "The cars are joined by the connecting passage. Someone will have to go out there, pull up the false floor, and unhitch the car."

"I think the choice is obvious," Rosalind said.

Charles nodded. He straightened his collar. With a shrug, he limped toward the door. "For King and Country," he said. "If I fall—"

"Not you!" Rosalind exclaimed, grabbing him by the jacket. "Me. I need you and Alix to shoot at them so they don't kill me."

"Ah, of course." Charles hesitated, but he did not argue. He smiled. "For the Stars and Stripes?"

"For Women's Suffrage," she replied without thinking,

unable to keep from smiling back. "But mostly for survival."

She pulled open the door and threw herself onto the
floor of the passage. Gunfire erupted—loud and scatter-
shot and terrifying, echoing with the cracks of impact on
the walls and baggage. Amid the noise, she heard Alix
call after her, "Rosalind! I am so very glad that we have
become friends! Please do not die!"

I hope I don't.

Rosalind's heart pounded in her ears. Bullets whizzed
back and forth over her head. Good thing she had paid some
attention to her father's sketches: she knew exactly where the
heavy metal pin was located—the one she needed to remove.
Keeping as low to the ground as she could manage, she pulled
up the floor panel to reach the coupling that connected the
two cars. Holding her breath, she reached down, wincing in
anticipation at each bump and bounce of the train. Then,
with as much desperation as courage, she yanked the metal
cylinder free.

"Pull the break!" she shouted, and grabbed for the
nearest railing.

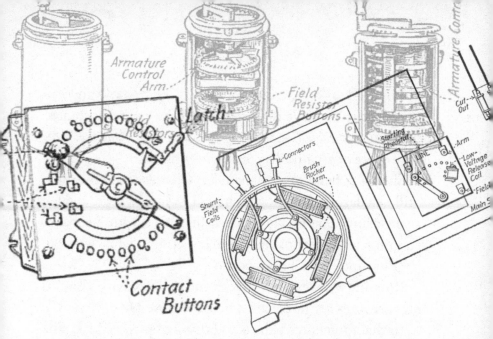

Armature
Control
Arm

Field
Resistor
Buttons

Armature Contr

Cut-
Out

Latch

Field
Resistors

Connectors

Starting
Rheostat

Arm

Low-
Voltage
Release
Coil

LINE

Brush
Rocker
Arm.

Shunt-
Field
Coils

Field

Main S

Contact
Buttons

The baggage car jolted with a violent lurch. Rosalind heard the unmistakable squeal of the breaks
engaging against the wheels at the very moment she
was flung forward by the force of the sudden stop.
Squeezing her eyes shut, she clung to the railing
with all her might. Her legs were thrown out from
under her and for a few horrible moments they
kicked helplessly in the air. Her fingers burned. If
she lost her grip, she would be dead: either from
the impact or crushed beneath the baggage car as it
skidded forward, slowing one bit at a time.

Finally, after an agonizing eternity that was
probably less than ten seconds, Rosalind fell
back onto the floor, numb and wide-eyed, as the
baggage car skidded to a halt in the center of
Columbia Station. Ahead of her, the train's roar
vanished into the tunnel. It was probably moving
even faster now . . . a good thing.

Chapter Eighteen

Rosalind sat on the edge of the car. Her gaze wandered to a large stone eagle that overlooked the tunnel entrance.

Damnable eagles, she thought. *Germany. America. One can't escape eagles anywhere, even under the ocean.*

She felt a hand on her shoulder: Charles stood over her. Still in a daze, she stood with his aid, swayed a little, and fell against him. She slowly touched his cheek with her hand, running her fingertips along it to be certain that he was real.

"Rosalind . . ." Charles began.

Rosalind rose onto her tiptoes and pulled Charles toward her, pressing her lips against his. She closed her eyes.

In that moment, all she could think of was the kiss. The kiss and Charles, and how well the two went together. Pulling away, she gazed into his eyes.

Then she slapped him across the face.

"I . . . What . . . ?" Charles stammered. He rubbed his cheek and looked at her hand, and then at her. "What was that for?"

"For bringing a bomb on my father's train and for getting Cecily killed," Rosalind said. "But not for the kiss. The kiss was lovely, if ill-timed."

"But you kissed *me*—"

"Bomb!" Alix shouted from behind them.

Rosalind and Charles exchanged another glance.

Charles released her and said, "Yes, right. Time to escape." He jumped to the ground and then took Rosalind by the waist and lifted her down. He did not, however, help Alix, who had to be helped down by Rosalind, after which Rosalind swatted Charles on the arm for being so rude.

"Now then, where are these submersibles?" Charles

wondered aloud, looking around. "Dear God, I do not believe it."

Rosalind followed his gaze. *Oh, no.* Bauer and his men were charging down the tunnel toward them. They must have decoupled their own car and made their way on foot.

"Run for it!" she shouted. She pushed Alix and Charles ahead of her and together they made for the nearest stair-case. Bauer's men began firing, though at that distance there was little fear of being hit. The more pressing concern was the bomb. Rosalind had no idea how long it had been since the timer was activated. Somehow they had to get to one of the subs before . . .

As she had that very thought, the baggage car exploded.

Rosalind was flung off her feet. The world turned to a deafening shower of fire and metal and disintegrated luggage. She struck the floor, hard. Dazed from the blast and the impact, she rolled onto her back and struggled to rise. The station spun around her. Funny: it was rather like Brandenburg Station, only with everything draped in red, white, and blue rather than black, white, and red.

No: it was exactly like the Brandenburg station, because the eagles were there, too.

Damnable eagles, indeed.

Turning away in disgust, she looked up at a great statue of Columbia: America personified as a beautiful woman draped in Greek robes, wearing a Phrygian cap, bearing the flag in one hand, her other hand outstretched—leading her people onward to claim new lands that probably didn't belong to them.

She looks like Mother, Rosalind realized. *Did Father do that on purpose? And why is the ceiling cracking?*

The force of the bomb had fractured the glass paneling in countless places. Even now, water was beginning to flow in. It was only a matter of time before the whole thing collapsed on top of them.

"Come along, Rosalind!" Alix shouted at her.

The girl grabbed Rosalind by the arm and pulled her to her feet. Charles lay a few paces away, also dazed, but he shook his head a few times and managed to stumble to his feet.

Rosalind grabbed Charles's hand and dragged him along behind her as she raced up the stairs with Alix. Below them, Bauer and his men began sloshing through the ankle-deep water. Two of the other men seemed injured; they lagged behind. But Bauer broke away from the pack and took the stairs two at a time.

Through the upstairs gallery she dashed with Charles and Alix past murals depicting the glories of Manifest Destiny.

"Rosalind," Alix said, "do you recall how you laughed at all the German pageantry in Brandenburg, and how you promised I could do the same here?"

"Yes?" Rosalind gasped, almost out of breath.

"Ha."

They turned a corner into the hallway with the escape subs. A bullet struck the wall behind Rosalind and ricocheted away. Glancing back, she saw Bauer throw his empty pistol away and clench his hands into fists.

Rosalind stopped at the nearest sub she could reach and began tugging on the airlock door's wheel. Charles joined her. Together they unlocked the door and heaved it open. The submersible inside was a long, boxy contraption shaped like a surface boat. It was furnished comfortably, almost like one of the lounges on the train, but with seats arranged in neat rows and only a few tables.

Not exactly the most efficient use of space, Rosalind noted, and she wondered just how many subs the station had to accommodate all of the passengers and crew. Because surely everyone was expected to be able to escape in an emergency, weren't they? But even as she posed the question to herself, she knew the answer. Survival was First Class Only.

Rosalind pushed Charles in first and then stumbled in after him. Unless this was part of Charles's spy training, she was the only person with any understanding of how the thing worked, so she would have to be the pilot. She dearly wished she had paid more attention when she had tested one with Father all those years ago.

Glancing back, she saw that Alix had not entered.

"Alix!" she cried. "Come on!"

"This is where we part company, Rosalind," Alix said, smiling pleasantly. "But do not worry, we will meet again. I do enjoy your company and I would like to have another philosophical discussion . . . under less trying circumstances, of course."

"Alix, what are you talking about?" Rosalind demanded, hurrying back through the sub toward the airlock. "There's plenty of room." She saw Bauer come into sight behind Alix and all but screamed, "Alix! Come on!"

"Safe journey, Rose," Alix said.

With that, she gave the door a shove. The last thing Rosalind saw before the airlock closed completely was Alix, smiling wickedly, slowly turning to face Bauer as she pulled a hatpin from her hair.

The door closed with a heavy clang.

"Alix!" Rosalind shouted again.

But it was too late.

At the helm, Charles strapped himself into one of the seats. He looked at the array of controls around him and held up his hands.

"I don't know what button to push," he said.

The urgency in his voice brought Rosalind back to the moment. Whatever became of Alix, they had to get away before the station collapsed.

She squeezed in next to Charles and looked over the controls. The array of brass levers, buttons, and dials were designed to confuse an intruder. Why someone would want to confuse anyone in the event of emergency, she hadn't realized until now—*Father might want everyone to sink*. She could just picture her father, poring over these details for security's sake. She took a deep breath, fighting to remember the launch sequence.

Top-right lever: up. Middle-level middle button: press. Bottom-middle dial: a turn to the left . . .

No.

She swallowed, ignoring Charles's stare. Father had designed the procedure out of sequence . . .

Top right lever: up. Bottom-middle dial: a turn to the left. Middle-level middle button: press—

The engine hummed to life. Water flooded the airlock.

"You did it, Rose," Charles said. He didn't sound surprised, or even relieved. He sounded as if this were expected.

The outer doors opened.

At that moment, she relaxed. Charles de Vere—the man, the fool, the aristocrat, the spy—had expected nothing less of her. So she'd deliver nothing less. She'd steered this type of vehicle plenty of times. With sure hands and feet on the levers and pedals, navigating thrust and attitude, she maneuvered the submersible out into the ocean and up toward the surface, always mindful of the pressure gauge.

At first she concentrated on getting clear of the station, but once they were safely away, a perverse curiosity overtook her. She twisted the craft around to watch Columbia in its death throes.

The glass panels gave way first, shattering in a chaotic torrent. Then, as the water poured in, the metal structure began to buckle. After that, the entire ceiling gave way, collapsing beneath the unstoppable weight of the ocean.

The observation lights on its surface flickered and went dim, leaving the station to die in darkness.

Rosalind's throat caught. Anger surged through her.

Goodbye, Alix, she said silently.

Struggling to focus, she activated the command to surface. As the submersible drifted upward through the dark water, she spotted movement. She craned her neck at an odd angle to catch sight of whatever it was. It was almost certainly another escape sub.

But who was aboard? Was it Alix? Or was it Bauer and his men?

As Rosalind watched, the other submersible seemed to set down on something dark and indistinct.

It took Rosalind a few more moments of staring to realize what she saw. It was the great, long beast she had observed from the train at the beginning of the journey.

The thing was not a whale. It was a submarine. A submarine larger than any Rosalind had ever heard of or certainly seen, larger than any she could even imagine.

She sat back in her chair, gripping the armrests. She tried to fathom who or what could have built a machine so large, and what they could possibly want.

A few minutes later, the submersible occupied by her and Charles broke through the water and into the air above.

Beside her, Charles gave a loud gasp of relief.

"My God," he said, "for a while there I feared I'd never see the surface again. Where are we?"

Rosalind took a few deep breaths herself and tried to make sense of things.

"We should be off the coast of Long Island," Rosalind said. She looked through the nearest windows and finally spotted the outline of land, barely visible against the starry sky.

"There," she said, pointing. "We should be able to make landfall within a few minutes."

"Hmm." Charles did not look pleased at that prospect. "What sort of distance can these things travel?"

Rosalind shrugged. "I have no idea, though they *are* designed to get people from the middle of the North Atlantic to land somewhere, so probably quite far."

"Could we make it to Canada?"

"I expect so," Rosalind said. She narrowed her eyes. "Why . . . ?"

"Under the circumstances, I think I'd rather not be answering any questions for the German or the American authorities. Not until I've had time to report in to my father."

"'Under the circumstances' . . ." Rosalind repeated.

"Yes?"

She shook her head. Her eyes fell. She stared at her hands. "I don't even know if the train reached New York in time. All those people might be dead because of us."

Charles rose from his chair and pulled Rosalind into his arms. "They must have," he assured her. "The train was moving so quickly, and it took a while for the station to flood. They'll be safe and sound, you'll see."

"I wish I believed that." Rosalind rested her cheek against Charles's shoulder. "I am *very* angry with you, Charles de Vere," she murmured. "I want you to know that."

"I'm not all that pleased with myself at the moment. I never intended for it to happen that way. And I certainly never meant for you to be dragged into it all or for Cecily to . . . to . . ." His voice quivered a little and he fell silent.

Rosalind held Charles, wondering to herself whether she dared ever trust him again. So many lies, so much deception. And yet, her feelings for him . . . She pulled away. Now was not the time for self-doubt. Now was the time for clear thinking.

"Charles . . ." she said.

"Mmm?"

"Do you suppose Alix was telling the truth about that second tunnel?"

There was a long pause and then Charles said, "I don't want it to be true, but I suspect that it is."

"That's what I thought."

She needed to know the truth. A pity her father wasn't there: she had questions for him, and she sorely wished to give him a piece of her mind. All of this was *his* fault. If it hadn't been for his damnable armaments scheme, none of this would have happened. Cecily and Doris would still be alive; she would be on her way home with them.

Only Father wasn't there. He was in New York, awaiting the triumphant arrival of his Transatlantic Express. He was in for a nasty surprise. But Rosalind doubted that even the loss of the railway would stop him for long. If there really was a second tunnel, nothing had changed. Father would still eagerly deliver American munitions to whatever European power needed them, even more eagerly now, with the legitimate business slowly sinking to the bottom of the Atlantic . . .

Father wouldn't just profit from war. Father would want one.

But perhaps there was a way for her to protest. And in the sweetest of ironies, Father's meticulous attention to detail would provide the means for her voice to be heard. All of the Transatlantic submersibles had been equipped with wireless transmitters to send distress calls.

Rosalind glanced at the control panel and quickly located the radio operator's station. She pulled away from Charles and switched the transmitter on.

"What are you doing?" Charles asked.

Rosalind scribbled a quick message on the operator's notepad and began transcribing it into Morse code. "I'm sending a letter to my father."

"You realize anyone listening to our frequency can intercept the message," Charles pointed out.

"Don't worry; I won't say anything about you."

Charles smirked. He placed his hand over hers. "I'm more concerned about you, Rose. The newspapers are bound to learn about this."

"I am counting on it," Rosalind told him.

She switched on the wireless and hesitated for a moment, her finger hovering over the key. Father was going to be furious at her. Who knew how he would react to being publicly rebuked by his own daughter? It was terrifying. But it was also liberating.

Steeling herself, Rosalind began to transmit:

To: Mr. Alexander Wallace
c/o the Transatlantic Railway Company
New York

Dear Father,
Warmest regards from the cold Atlantic. My stay in London was wonderful. My journey on your train was not. I have given your best wishes to Lord and Lady Exham, but they are unable to return them, having just suffered a horrifying tragedy. They have you to thank for it. Your secret is not as safe as you thought it was.

Thank you for the ticket on the Transatlantic Express. I wore a hat and dressed respectably. I was nearly killed. Was that part of being the family's representative?

I know what you are doing.

Your loving daughter,
Rosalind

P.S. The public will judge you.

Rosalind repeated the message three times for good measure before sinking back into her chair in a sort of daze. She should have been terrified. Perhaps she was terrified. But she was also elated, dizzy with excitement. This *was* freedom—release from the anger she felt at the lies and betrayal and murder through a single message to the man responsible for it all.

Beside her, Charles looked over the message. He blinked a few times, and then he placed a hand on her shoulder.

"Your father will be furious at this," he said.

"I am counting on that, too."

"He might disown you."

"I don't care. I don't care anymore." Rosalind looked at Charles, her hands clenched into fists. "If he was willing to transport armaments—"

"He's not the man you thought he was?" Charles ventured.

Rosalind shook her head. "He is exactly the man I thought he was: a vicious, self-serving profiteer. All my life I have been lying to myself about that. I think I'm finally admitting what I knew all along."

"Do you think there really is a second tunnel?"

"Only one way to find out," Rosalind said. "Have a seat. We are going investigating."

Charles strapped himself into his chair. "Are you certain about this?" he asked, but he'd started to smile.

"Not particularly," Rosalind said, pressing on the lever for descent as the blue-green water rushed up over the windows. "But I want some answers. It seems the only way I'm getting them is by finding them myself."

And with that, she plunged the submersible back into the murky depths.

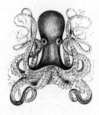